MS#1705StopRape/65,041 words
April 14, 2014

StopRape.com

A novel by

Harley L. Sachs

Paper ISBN 9781939381415
Ebook ISBN 9781939381422

Books by Harley L. Sachs:

Novels

Queer Company
Never Trust a Talking Horse
The Gold Chromosome
Murder by Mail (Scratch—out!)!
Ben Zakkai's Coffin
The Search for Jesse Bram
The Mystery Club Solves a Murder
The Mystery Club and the Dead Doctor
The Mystery Club and the Hidden Witness
The Mystery Club and the Serial Widow
Deliver me from Evil
White Slave
Conspiracy!
Murder in the Keweenaw
The Lollipop Murder
Betrayal
Retribution
Burnt Out
Sam in Love
StopRape.com

Collections of short fiction

Ahoy! Quarterdeck! (Irma Quarterdeck Reports)
Anna-Lena's Troll and other stories
Threads of the Covenant: The Jews of Red Jacket
Misplaced Persons

Non-Fiction

Freelance Non-Fiction Articles
The Misadventures of Cpl. Sachs
The 1957 Sachs Arctic Expedition
From Tent to Castle: Memoir of a Year-Long Honeymoon
IS
Chilly-Chilly BANG! How We Freelanced Through Europe's Coldest Winter in a VW with a Kid
Essays and Columns: 1992-2011
The Writing Life

Cartoons

Hunting the Mail Buoy and other hazards to navigation

Dedicated to all victims of rape and abuse.

"When law and order fail, the last resort is revenge."
--- Hillel ben Jakov

Chapter One: The Interview

She came into the WMUP television station totally
unannounced and unexpected. She was tall with a physique
that might have qualified her for a high school football team
if they let girls play, so it was no surprise when she told me
she had enlisted in the Marine Corps. How different the
military was since I was a kid, which wasn't that long ago, I
hoped.

At first I thought she might have been deployed in
Afghanistan or Iraq or one of those places we keep sending
kids into harm's way because she had that look about her that
said she had PTSD, some trauma. I thought she might have
been blown up by an IED, or in a helicopter that crashed, but
it turned out to be none of the above. She hadn't been
deployed. She hadn't been wounded. She hadn't even
finished basic training. She'd been raped by her drill sergeant.

That explained a lot, but not why she'd come to WMUP.
I figured that most women who were assaulted didn't want to
talk about it. She wanted more than just talk.

Rape in the military is a major problem and it's not just
women who are sexually assaulted. She explained that men
can be raped, too. The number of sexual assaults on males is
almost as great as on women, but of course proportionally
the women get the worst of it. It's a national scandal. It's not
only boy scouts and choir boys who have been victims.

She'd reported the rape to the commanding officer and
he'd blown her off. Typical. So, unable to work, she left the
marines with PTSD, a medical discharge, honorable, and here
she was at my desk.

I was taking notes by that time, but she wouldn't tell me her full name. She said she was "Maggie," and if I interviewed her I was not to show her face. If possible, she wanted her voice altered.

She wanted to talk about her campaign against rape. She had a web site called StopRape.com. That was the meat of her story.

For permission to do the interview I had to consult with the boss, Queen Annie, the station owner and manager. Queen Annie is a no nonsense person who respects a subject's need for privacy, and to my surprise she consented. So we did it.

We would tape the interview and edit it for the evening broadcast or whenever it wasn't preempted by some national disaster. Since it was recorded in the studio, it would be a two camera setup, one on me, the other on her. I got the high sign and we were on.

When she saw that the red light on the TV camera was on, our subject knew we were recording. Because she wanted to be anonymous, we had to do it with her head silhouetted against a painted Upper Michigan forest scene backdrop in the WMUP studio.

Michigan is divided into two peninsulas, the LP and the UP, land of the Yoopers. About a third of the UP residents are of Finnish extraction, which includes me. I guess the Finns came to this part of the country because it looks just like Finland, complete with lakes and mosquitoes.

Because Finnish doesn't have prepositions, local people say things like "We go Green Bay, watch Packers play" or "We go sauna, hey." I have to be careful not to fall into that speech pattern, hey, especially when I'm on camera. Ours is a small, local TV station, an NBC affiliate, and most of what goes on over the cable is network stuff, but this interview was a potentially hot story, and I had the first shot at it.

I risked that if it got very heavy attention, Network would snatch it away from us and hand the story over to the big boys. After all, as Kerstin Mikkola, a not so beautiful grad from TV school at NMU in Michigan's remote Upper Peninsula, I don't have a lot of prestige. And I'm not blonde with big boobs. Still, maybe this could be my ticket to something bigger than a small Yooper station.

The WMUP studio is in the old terminal of a now virtually abandoned airport. We used to get jet airliners in here, but they've all been moved to the old K.I. Sawyer air force base a few miles away. Now only private planes land here.

The fact that airliners no longer land at the old airport killed a nearby motel that catered to passengers. That's how I got my apartment. The motel owner decided to cut his losses and convert the rooms into small apartments, so I got a one bedroom, living room and kitchen at a reasonable price. Of course, it's on the ground floor. As a single woman I'd feel safer if it weren't so accessible. There's no garage, of course, so my Taurus is parked outside in the snow. Here in the sub-arctic UP that means six months of the year.

At least the job at WMUP was a step up from my first job at the Ojibwa reservation. I used to do radio news broadcasts out of the Chinook Winds casino in Christmas, Michigan. I'm not Native American, so I lost that one. But there isn't much future at WMUP, either. The interview with the gal from StopRape.com could be my ticket out of here.

Here's the transcript of what eventually went out on the air:

"I'm Kerstin Mikkola and we're in the studio of WMUP. Today we're interviewing Maggie, not her real name. She is an ex-marine recruit who claims to have been raped while in basic training at Fort Ord, California. She is the host of the controversial web site "StopRape.Com."

Q. Maggie, isn't your web site similar to StopRapeNow?"

A. StopRapeNow is a United Nations program with examples of attacks on women all over the world. Though the purpose of my web site is to stop rapes, it goes directly to the perpetrators. StopRape.com is like those web sites that post the pictures and details of convicted child molesters and wanted criminals. The FBI posts the Ten Most Wanted. My site posts the pictures of rapists.

Q. These are convicted rapists, Right?

A. Not necessarily. As my web site always cautions, unless they were convicted, these are alleged rapists. I do that just as your station is always careful to use the term "alleged" to avoid law suits for defamation and libel. It's not so very different from newspapers publishing the names of johns arrested for soliciting prostitutes.

Q. I heard that when mayors, public officials, the clergy have had their names published for being arrested for consorting with hookers, they've threatened to sue.

A. You have to understand, the information posted on my web site comes from the paid subscribers. They are solely responsible for the veracity of the content of what they post. It's in the contract.

Q In the contract?

A Yes, when you access my site to upload your content, you have to agree to the legal contract.

Q. But nobody ever reads those agreements.

A. My responsibility it to state the issues clearly. If people don't read the agreement, that's their problem, not mine.

Q. I haven't read it, either. Just what do they agree to?

A. They agree that they are solely responsible for the veracity of what they post to the web site, that they are not to use it to slander or libel anyone, and that in case of suits for damages, they are solely responsible. We are no more liable for the content than the wall some tagger writes an obscenity on.

Q. But the owner of such a wall may have to paint over the obscenity.

A. Sure. If we find that something posted was illegal, slanderous, or libelous, we take it down.

Q. So anyone can post the picture and personal data of a convicted rapist?

A. They don't have to be convicted. Since most rapes are never reported to the police, StopRape.com gives victims the opportunity to report anonymously.

Q. Anonymously? But you have to know the identity of the accuser.

A. Of course.

Q How do you know the source is truthful?

A. We have to take their word for it.

Q. So these are alleged rapists? Don't you need collaborative evidence?

A. How can you if there are no witnesses? Some of these cases in court break down to he said/she said. I admit it is a gray area. They are all alleged until proven guilty in a court of law.

Q. Sounds like someone with a bone to pick could call anyone a rapist.

A. They'd better not.

Q. How long as your site been up?

A. Several months.

Q. How many hits has your web site attracted?

A, Thousands, so far, and we have over a hundred postings of rapists on our Wall of Shame.

Q. What goes into a posting?

A. Pictures of the perps, their addresses, even photos of their homes, just like the posting made on anti-abortionists' sites.

Q. Heavy stuff.

At this point I wasn't sure where I wanted to go next, and the director was pointing at the studio clock. I would have gladly carried on for an hour, but had to wrap it up.

Preliminary to the broadcast interview "Maggie" kept talking, going on and on about rape in the military. She pointed out in details I didn't want to hear, men can be raped, that rape is defined as illegal penetration, and that can be done with a broom handle or a coke bottle or worse. The point she made was that rape was not just a sexual act, but a brutal assault to humiliate the victim.

She went into gory detail about her own rape. She'd injured her shoulder in training and was staying alone in the barracks when the drill sergeant came in and climbed onto her. Her injured shoulder made it impossible for her to defend herself. The company commander's attitude was, "Boys will be boys. It's just excessive testosterone. Normal behavior."

But rape is not normal behavior. It's a power play. Until the rape she had been one of the outstanding trainees. Afterwards, her performance dropped. Ultimately she couldn't function at all and was discharged. She was depressed, angry, but she did not blame herself. She wasn't going to fall for that psychological trap. She wanted to get even.

So now that she was out of the military, she set up StopRape.com. The object was to show that rape was a step in a continuum of violence that could begin with mere bullying.

Our cameraman, Eino, an Upper Peninsula Finnlander, joked that bullying begins with nagging, that his wife was always nagging him, and could that be a precursor to rape?

Eino is a good guy, but he's reached his level of competence. He's about fifty, not in very good health, and has been with WMUP since it was started. He was hired by Queen Annie's now deceased husband, so he's been around that long. The bulky TV camera we lug around on shoots is getting to be too much for him.

I told him to lock up the brooms at home and watch out. He didn't think it was funny.

I didn't want to go into the details of her rape on our news broadcast and told her so before the interview. Before she left the studio she insisted, for legal reasons, that she be provided with a DVD of the interview. She said she wanted evidence if she were misrepresented by the edit, but that we shouldn't think of her request as a demand for prior restraint. That would be a violation of first amendment rights and journalistic ethics.

I didn't think Queen Annie would approve, but I saw no harm in it, and foolishly gave "Maggie" a quick and dirty digital copy of the entire interview for her files. She left the station and that was the last I saw of her. Saw, but not heard. There was plenty to come.

As I feared, when it came to the editing of the interview for the actual broadcast, it got cut down to under a minute. The subject was too graphic for the six o'clock dinner time news. It ended up on the ten o'clock just after a piece about a bear that got into someone's back porch garbage and the weather report. So much for my ticket to fame as a TV interviewer.

Or so I thought.

Chapter Two: Then came the Mail

When I drove up to the station in my old Ford Taurus a couple of days later I found a bundle of letters in a rubber band on my sometimes desk. They were all responses to that brief late evening broadcast. There were a couple of crudely written, anguished notes from tormented women who claimed to have been raped and needed help, but were too embarrassed to go public about it.

What did they expect me to do? Counsel them?

There was also a threat from a man who said he'd been wrongly accused. His picture was on the Wall of Shame, he said, but he had never been arrested. He knew who had uploaded his picture. He claimed she had been drunk at the time and that the sex was consensual. He demanded that his picture be taken down. Or else.

There was no explanation of what "or else" meant.

I didn't have the authority or the means to remove him from "Maggie's" wall of shame. I looked for his face on the StopRape.com web site. Sure enough, he was here. He looked like anybody else you might see on the street, but from what my sheriff's deputy boy friend Charlie says, they all do.

I didn't have the home address for "Maggie," but the web site provided a post office address and I sent all the mail to it. I didn't want any of that stuff hanging around. For my own insurance, to cover my ass, I probably should have made copies for my file, but I didn't.

As for the StopRape web site, it's a two level deal, like what you see if you get a peek at the New York Times web site. You can get a teaser preview, but to post your own rapist's picture and to read the full dossiers of the accused you have to subscribe. To do that I'd have to send five dollars in dues to a Paypal account. Not sure of the confidentiality of the list, I didn't want to be identified as a subscriber, but I took a chance and paid up.

In a banner across the top of the StopRape web page is a disturbing quotation: "When Law and Order Fail, the last resort for justice is revenge."—Hillel ben Jakov.

I didn't know who Hillel ben Jakov was, but it sounded like a rabbi or something in the Bible.

Was StopRape.com intended as an incitement for revenge or just a statement of fact? The more I thought about that the scarier it got. Revenge was what motivated tribal wars in Afghanistan. Revenge was what the relatives of victims of drone strikes in Pakistan wanted against the United States. They couldn't take a drone to court or find the kid who pushed the remote control button that launched the smart bomb from thousands of miles away, so what was left?

Then the shit hit the fan.

I got called into the station manager's office. Queen Annie is a fifty-ish woman who may have been the widow of the original station owner, but was obviously the brains of the outfit. Queen Annie is a Yooper like me, which might explain her rough lumberjack style of clothing, but she still couldn't dress like that if she weren't the boss. She is the boss, and she can smoke those little cigars in the office and wear anything she likes, like the frown she was aiming at me when I came in. You can't smoke in most places nowadays, but nobody would dare tell her not to smoke in the office. It's her place, hey.

Annie had a sentimental attachment to some old things, like she uses an antique Zippo lighter for her cigars. She even keeps an old dial telephone from the days when ma Bell offered only one color—black. She has it mounted on an ash tray base like some novelty. Queen Annie has a big flat screen monitor on her computer and she had it logged in to U-Tube.

My God, there was my video interview, not just the 60 second edit, but the whole thing, uncut but embellished. Maggie must have a videographer available, for the twelve minute result was slick and guaranteed to go viral.

For me the tough part was seeing my own face on U-Tube. TV cameras make you look fat, which I am not, but the distortion can be distressing. I have to do something about my hair. With me every day is a bad hair day. I don't know if I should have it cut short, wear it in a pony tail, tease it up high on my head or what. Sometimes I think I should just get a wig that always looks good. I was still pondering about my hair when it got to the end of the video.

At the end the camera zoomed in on an offer that went with each subscription: a free "Rapist" sticker the alleged victim could sneak onto the bumper of the car driven by the alleged perp. I hadn't seen that on the web site.

I wondered if those were easy to peel off or if they permanently damaged the paint.

Queen Annie demanded, "Did you give her the tape of the interview?"

I apologized. "She wanted it for legal purposes in case we misquoted her."

"She sounds litigious." Queen Annie set down her cigar on a souvenir Ojibwa casino ashtray and sipped her cup of coffee, a mug with the station logo. "At least she left in the brief shot of your face and the mention of the station. Free advertising for us."

Or me. Sensing an unnerving chilling effect, I added, "Mine is the only face that actually shows in the video. It makes it look like I'm the sponsor of StopRape.com and not just a TV interviewer."

Queen Annie smiled. She's had teeth implants, a perfect set. "Your moment of fame, Mikkola. Just remind people that we report the news. We don't create it."

I wasn't so sure about that. Once something gets on U-Tube it becomes news.

I knew that anchors like Diane Sawyer can become celebrities themselves, better known than the people they interview. I didn't think I wanted to be a celebrity connected to StopRape.com.

"Good for the station," Annie said. "How many subscribers do you think we have on the cable? Thirty thousand? If this U-Tube thing goes viral, millions will hear about us."

"You mean about me."

Annie's cigar had gone out. She relit it with that Zippo lighter. "Did you subscribe to the lady's web site?"

"Actually, I did. I wanted to get the full story in case of a follow-up."

"Good idea to get a better handle on it, just in case."

"In case what?"

Queen Annie likes to intimidate people. It's her management style. "You never know. Sometimes there are surprises."

The only surprises I like are at Christmas when Santa brings me something I really wanted.

Annie was right. Surprises were coming.

Chapter Three: Bumper stickers

In due time my membership packet to StopRape.com arrived by snail mail in an innocuous plain manila envelope including two rapist bumper stickers. I wasn't about to use my option to post the face or name of any alleged rapist. Thank God I haven't been raped, though the statistics are that one in every four or five women have been sexually abused at one time or another.

I showed the bumper sticker to my sometimes boy friend, Charlie Johnson. He's a Finnlander, too, like many of us Yoopers, but his great granddad took a Swedish sounding name to get a better job in the mines in those days. Back then the Finns got the worst jobs and the Swedes were foremen. The Welsh miners were the elite.

I met Charlie when Eino and I went out to get some shots of a major wreck on the highway. Charlie was on duty, looking great in his uniform and Smoky Bear hat. He had seen me on the evening news and came on to me as if worshipping a major star. It was flattering, and we dated.

Charlie started out as a prison guard for one of our minimum security prisons, then moved up. The trolls below the Mackinac Bridge don't want prisoners in their own back yard, so the U.P. is the Michigan Gulag. It's a sad fact that a disproportionate number of our inmates are African-American and poor. If they come from the Detroit area and do their time in the Upper Peninsula their families never get to visit. It's hundreds of mile away and public transportation is crap.

Charlie had a job at the Marquette prison for awhile, what the offenders sometimes call Granite University. He got out of there and is now a sheriff's deputy. He's a good-hearted guy, a bit cynical at times, which is hard to avoid if you'd had to stand over the scum of the earth.

He was over at my place one night for pizza, beer, and a cuddle. We had reached the heavy breathing stage when his pager went off and he got called out on an emergency. I swore right then that I would never marry a cop. Coitus interruptus is not my idea of romance or satisfactory sex. If you'll pardon the pun, screw it.

But we're pals, and it's helpful for a TV news reporter to have an in with the police. Beats just listening to a scanner and trying to decipher the codes the sheriff invents to befuddle the local violators.

I showed Charlie the StopRape.com bumper sticker. "What would you do if you found one of these on your jeep?"

Charlie had just got off duty and was wearing his uniform complete with taser, handcuffs, and his pet Glock. He gave me a suspicious squint. "I'd be pissed."

"Yeh, but what would you do about it?"

"Peel it off, for one."

"This wouldn't peel so easily," I said. "Take a look. It's made to break into separate bits. But aside from removing it, then what?"

Charlie rolled his eyes back as he did a mental search for definitions of violations. "Find out who did it."

"No fingerprints," I said.

"It's vandalism. Not more than a misdemeanor at most. Judge wouldn't do anything about it."

"Not a case for slander, libel, or defamation?"

Charlie shook his head. "If someone stuck a baby killer sticker on an abortionist's bumper it would be about the same. Just an irritant."

"So? Then it's harmless."

Charlie shrugged. "Depends on how thin-skinned you are when someone calls you names. Look, we can't even catch up with people who slash tires, and that's a lot more serious. Tires cost money, and malicious destruction of property over $100 can get you some jail time."

I didn't think any judge would give jail time for that, considering how full of wife beaters and child molesters our jails are.

Charlie agreed. "But you have to have evidence, like video surveillance. You could probably stick one of these rapist signs on while pretending to tie your shoe in the parking lot. Nobody would notice, even if there were cameras everywhere."

I slipped the sticker back into the plain manila envelope it came in. "Then it's a harmless irritant, an embarrassment."

Charlie nodded. "I think your StopRape lady is blowing smoke out her ass. The stickers are just going to give some victims a chance to get back at the perps."

I was worried. "I don't know, Charlie. I've seen the photos of those bums on the web site. You told me once that many people are just a six pack away from a capital crime. A bumper sticker might set someone off."

"Just don't get any ideas about putting one on my jeep."

"It'd never do that to you, Charlie."

He didn't look like he was so sure.

Harley l. Sachs

Chapter four: The Beat Goes On.

I didn't think much more about Maggie's web site. With us on TV if it bleeds it leads, and there was no blood in this story.

Now that I was a so-called subscriber to StopRape.com I could check out the postings. There were dozens and from all over the country. One stuck out because it was so complete. It posted not only the photograph of a Marine sergeant in uniform, but a picture of his car with the California license plate showing and his house. He lived in San Diego in a manufactured home with his wife and two kids. It was like a whole dossier. His name was Carlos Wayne Sauvenier. Sounded like a hybrid wine.

The chill came when I got to the narration of his alleged rape. He had assaulted a female trainee in the barracks where she had been resting after hurting her shoulder. The victim had reported the crime and had been blown off by the commanding officer. Sauvenier had to be the guy the woman who called herself Maggie had told me about. This was Maggie's way of saying, "Gotcha!" But Sauvenier was in California, not the U.P. of Michigan. I assumed that Maggie lived somewhere up here in the UP, not in California. Maybe he wasn't the guy after all.

There were so many other posted pictures of bad guys I didn't see that she could accomplish anything. Women being assaulted by boy friends, husbands, and strangers, that it was near to acceptance as normal behavior by testosterone fired dick heads. It didn't help that cops had a way of shrugging off those assaults, claiming women dressed provocatively, got what they deserved, yadda, yadda, yadda.

What I did do was set up a search on the free Giga Alert internet clipping service. I had already done that for my name, so any time Kerstin Mikkola shows up anywhere in the world, I get an email notification. To stay abreast of the

19

StopRape story I set up a Giga Alert for the web site to see what action might take place.

Then I googled Carlos Wayne Sauvenier. It's not a common name and aside from getting directed to the posting at StopRape.com there was nothing.

The picture of Sauvenier that was put up on the web site was of a mean-looking white guy with a shaved head, no neck, and a sneer on his face. The only thing missing might be a Hell's Angels biker's jacket. This was a person I would have avoided at any time.

At the station my camera man Eino and I got sent out on wildlife stories like the buck that jumped through someone's picture window and rampaged through the house trying to get out again. Then there was the yearling bear that had to be coaxed down out of a tree in town with a tranquilizer dart shot by the DNR. In the big cities those stories are about puppies and pussycats that get in trouble, or some old lady who keeps fifty cats. People can relate to those stories better than something in the international political news. Those stories are for the network anyway. I forgot about Carlos Wayne Sauvenier. He was just another jerk with a dick. There were plenty of those around.

Then I got a surprise visit from a man in a topcoat and cheap three piece dark suit. He flashed an ID that said "G. Marshall, FBI."

"You Kerstin Mikkola?"

"Sure. What's this about?"

"What do you know about this man?" He showed me a picture I recognized. It was the same shot that was on the web site. Carlos Wayne Sauvenier.

"He's an alleged rapist," I said. "That's the picture posted at StopRape.com."

"We're investigating a hate crime."

"Not a rape? Are you're finally going to prosecute him? Did you have to wait until he got denounced on the World Wide Web?"

"No. He's the victim."

"Poor baby," I said with heavy sarcasm, for I remembered the details of his brutal rape. "What happened?"

"He was castrated."

Ooo, nasty. So there was blood in this story after all, but not the sort suitable for the six-o'clock dinner broadcast. If some rapist in California gets his cajones snipped, that's not Yooper news.

There was more. "His scrotum was nailed up above the door of his house under a sticker that says 'Rapist.'"

No doubt the rapist sticker was the link.

I shook my head. "Wow. And Sauvenier isn't even black. I thought that went out with lynching. What's that got to do with me?"

At WMUP we don't see many visitors in three piece suits. At the most this is a sport jacket place and only if the person wearing one is on camera. The visitor had attracted the attention of others at the studio. Eino was hanging around, obviously eavesdropping.

I had no sympathy for sergeant Sauvenier. For his wife, maybe, but I remembered they already had two kids. They wouldn't be having any more. "So what do you want from me? We did an interview about the StopRape web site weeks ago. Maybe we can do a follow-up." I couldn't imagine Queen Annie going for it. I teased, "Want to be on TV?"

G. Marshall, FBI definitely did not want to be on TV. "I want to know who runs the StopRape web site, who posted Sauvenier's alleged rape on it."

My fourth estate instincts kicked in. Journalists aren't required to reveal their sources. "I can't tell you that."

G. Marshall's eyes narrowed in an attempt to intimidate me. "You won't?"

"I wouldn't even if I knew. If you did your homework you must have seen the U-tube video, which is probably why you've come to me because I'm in it."

His facial expression told me I'd guessed right.

I explained, "We never knew the woman's real name. She called herself Maggie and insisted on not showing her face. We even had to disguise her voice. She's very sensitive about being identified."

"Why's that?"

I surreptitiously wrote gown G. Marshall's name on a note pad so I wouldn't forget. "She's obviously afraid of reprisals. As the host of StopRape.com you can imagine that the men whose names are posted will want to get even. Identifying and denouncing criminals can be dangerous. They hate rats." That's the term I learned from Charlie's old job at the prison.

Marshall was thoughtful. "Can you describe her for me?"

I could do that much. "She's a big girl, not fat or overweight, just an athletic build. Her hair was short, like she was butch." Remembering how she looked, and the picture of Sauvenier, I could imagine that he thought she was a dyke. She looked tough. She'd have made a tough marine, maybe too tough, a challenge for the drill sergeant. Maybe Sauvenier resented her, was homophobic, and wanted to teach her a lesson. Rape, after all, is a crime of violence to humiliate the victim and make them submissive. It's not just about sex. I didn't have to explain that to G. Marshall.

Marshall was running down his shopping list for a description. "What about her features? Hair color? Eyes? Any tattoos?"

"No visible tattoos," I said. "She was wearing winter clothes, slacks, and long sleeves so I wouldn't have seen if she had any. Brown hair, dark eyes."

Agent Marshall wrote things down on a little pocket notebook. "Anything else?"

I rubbed my nose. "I don't know if this fits your requirement for a physical description, but she doesn't smile. I think the most she'd muster would be a chagrined grin. She's bitter."

G. Marshall wrote something. "Uh huh."

"Well, you would, too if you were raped and nobody paid you any attention."

He seemed to agree.

"So if you locate this Maggie person, what are you going to do, arrest her for assaulting Sauvenier? I doubt she was in California."

He shook his head. "More likely charge the lady with conspiracy."

"That's a stretch. Put up pictures of alleged criminals on the World Wide Web and suddenly it's a conspiracy? That the FBI posts pictures of the ten most wanted doesn't make it a government conspiracy against criminals."

He agreed and changed tactics. "You recognized the Sauvenier photo from the web site. You a subscriber?"

"Sure. It's part of my investigative reporting, like when the FBI joins the Communist Party to find out what goes on at the meetings. Just because I own a copy of the Koran doesn't make me a Muslim."

"OK." Marshall wasn't getting anyplace.

"And don't expect me to reveal my sources. It's a First Amendment thing."

Marshall put away his little notebook. "If you withhold evidence you can be held in contempt of court."

Now who was blowing smoke? I insisted, "I'm just an unimportant Upper Peninsula TV reporter." I gestured at Eino. "Eino here and I chase lost bears in people's back yards. I don't have evidence of any conspiracy."

The fact is, I did, but I wasn't going to tell him that.

Chapter Five: And there's more

Agent Marshall was pussyfooting around my fourth estate rights. "How do you get in touch with the woman from StopRape.com?"

"I forward the hate mail to the post office box posted on the web site."

"OK. The post office box is in a suburb of Minneapolis. You knew that, of course."

"I guess I did. I hadn't thought about it." That was puzzling. If the StopRape post office box was in Minnesota, why did she show up at WMUP in the Upper Peninsula of Michigan? Didn't make sense. Minneapolis had bigger stations than ours. Maybe, because WMUP is so small, she might have figured we were hungry for a story that a big city station wouldn't be bothered with. Still, WMUP is a long day's drive from Minneapolis, and this is winter. Those miles of roads through the forest are a bad place to get stuck. I had just assumed she was local. I didn't find out about the PO address until after the interview. Then I was too busy to think about it.

G. Marshall continued with his interrogation. "How did you contact her for the TV interview?"

"She just walked in one day, cold."

"She have a phone?"

"Probably, but I don't know the number. There's a contact us email address on the web site. You must know that already. You could track her down that way."

Marshall nodded. "She's probably funneling all her emails through TOR."

"What's that?"

"TOR is a pool of computers that relay emails so they can't be traced."

Deciphering the email headers was beyond my rudimentary computer skills. It's hard to be anonymous on the Internet, but "Maggie" was doing her best. "I bet the web site host knows or they couldn't set up the service."

"That can be done anonymously," Agent Marshall said. "You can build a false identity. You can be anybody. I could be Kerstin Mikkola."

"I don't think my wardrobe would fit you."

What with identify theft, our fastest growing crime, I supposed he could be right. Then I realized the FBI wanted a face to face meeting, maybe to arrest the lady.

G. Marshall, FBI, seemed satisfied that I knew nothing. He gave me his card with his cell phone number and left, watched by Queen Annie from her office lair. As soon as he was gone she came out. Annie has a sort of swagger you might expect from someone who has a concealed weapons carry permit, but she doesn't. She doesn't need a firearm to intimidate anyone. "What was that about?"

I held up the business card. "Says he is G. Marshall, FBI. Wants to know who we interviewed on that StopRape segment. How about that, hey?"

Now her interest was piqued. She smelled a story. "More."

"I'm pretty sure that the marine who raped our subject was castrated out in San Diego."

"Coincidence?"

I shook my head. "G. Marshall seems to have a conspiracy theory going."

Queen Annie gave me one of her cynical smiles. "Maybe we should tell him about the latest Yooper UFO sightings."

I stuck the business card in the corner of the old-fashioned desk blotter, a relic from the days of fountain pens and ink. I guessed the FBI must be short of terrorists, pot growers, and meth cookers, but then those are for the alcohol, firearms, and drug teams.

Queen Annie went back to her office, but the whole conspiracy thing got me thinking. I was reminded of that Hillel ben Jakov quotation so prominently placed on the StopRape web site. "When law and order fail, the last resort is revenge." Maybe this Maggie person's intention was to rabble rouse rape victims to do more than just denounce the scum bags, but actually take more serious action than putting stickers on the bumpers of their cars, serious action like cutting off their testicles.

Maggie was no longer in the military, but she might still have friends. Maybe there was a band of sisters at the base near in San Diego, a kind of vigilante group. Now that was a possible conspiracy. G. Marshall might not be so wacko after all. I resolved to watch the web site pretty closely.

It's a pretty extensive site. There are chat groups and discussions, and tactics, like how to make sure that rape kits aren't just stored forever in some evidence room and never analyzed, thereby giving serial rapists a free ride for more violence against women.

There's medical advice, "What to do if you've been raped," and legal advice. A pro bono lawyer moderates that part of the site.

I was beginning to develop a genuine admiration for Maggie's pluck. She might have been assaulted in the military but she had guts. Like the Marines say, *semper fi.*, always ready. StopRape.com was a counterattack in the war against women in general. Good for her.

So I wondered, did someone back at the base subscribe to the site and organize a castration party? The Rapist sticker suggested there was. And was G. Marshall right in claiming this was a hate crime? Hating men might be a new category, a turnabout from misogyny. It wasn't legal to go around mutilating people no matter how much they might deserve it. There had to be law and order, but if law and order failed…

I googled Sauvenier's name again. This time I got a link to a newspaper story. It was pretty awful. Sergeant Sauvenier had been drinking and was lured out into the parking lot of a bar where several attackers subdued him. He'd been pretty drunk, couldn't identify the woman who suggested they have sex at her place. When he came to he'd been dumped on his front steps without his pants or his balls.

The attack had taken place out of sight of any surveillance cameras. There were none outside his trailer, either, so there were no witnesses to the nailing of his scrotum over his own front door. Mrs. Sauvenier must have been a sound sleeper.

Sauvenier was a tough guy. Clearly it had taken more than one person to do this.

According to the newspaper report, the investigation was ongoing. A sidebar mentioned that Sauvenier had been accused of rape, but never charged because the commanding officer threw out the complaint. So much for the Universal Code of Military justice.

Obviously Maggie had sisters in arms, and I was sure nobody was going to tell. Just to make it more difficult to follow up with an investigation, the unit had been deployed abroad. In war-torn eastern countries there were more serious injuries than mere castration.

I returned to the StopRape chat lines. I knew that G. Marshall and his cohorts, probably the NSA, which watches everybody, would be paying attention to all the chatter on the web site. I didn't have confidence that limiting access to the chat room to "friends" or "members only" would withstand the NSA snoops. Like the FBI, they could always pose as being a "friend." But I didn't have to simply lurk in silence. I had a legitimate reason to be visiting the site, especially since I was the star of the U-tube video. Just because I was a subscriber didn't mean I was a co-conspirator.

So I put in a comment on Sauvenier. I didn't suggest that I knew who was being avenged. That was my educated guess.

There were other aspects to the case even if he hadn't been emasculated. If he was actually tried for the rape in the first place, and if he was acquitted, his name was out there as having been accused. The stain "accused rapist" would not go away. Google would find it.

If he had been convicted and given a wrist slap, like loss of one stripe and thirty days in the brig, he might have had to register as a sex offender. His thirty days in the joint, as Charlie calls it, might be up, and he might even be forced to do community service cleaning toilets, but once you're a registered sexual predator, it's twenty-five years, practically a life sentence. Could he be allowed to live in a house with his own children? Probably, since it wasn't kiddy porn he was accused of.

The trauma of being raped doesn't go away. Nor was Sergeant Sauvenier going to grow a new set of testicles, either. I wondered what would happen to him next.

I told Queen Annie about it. She lolled back in her old swivel chair like the Wise Woman of the Mountain. "I don't want rape stories. They plant ideas in the heads of copycats. You can start a crime wave by reporting on certain crimes. Look at what happens when there's a shooter."

I didn't see a connection.

"All those pictures of family members crying, flowers and teddy bears as memorials. Makes a big show, makes the shooter a famous person. We don't want to encourage crime."

"What about suicide by cop?" I suggested.

"That, too."

Clearly Queen Annie, though she was in the news business, preferred the replays of high school football games to reminders of the miserable lives of some people here in the U.P. She wasn't in the news business to be a muckraker or social crusader. Running the brief interview about StopRape.com was about as far as she'd go. That was a women's rights issue, and in spite of her macho Yooper looks, Annie is a woman.

She wasn't going to pursue the StopRape story and encourage copycat rapists, but I was hooked. I just knew in my guts that Sauvenier's castration was the beginning of something, maybe worse.

Chapter Six: What Next?

The live chat on the web site was far ranging from responses like "Yah, right," to longer ventings of frustration and anger.

Then there was the pitiful case of Waldo, a pimply seventeen year old high school football star who had sex with his fourteen year old girl friend. The girl might have been the high school slut, but she was under age, and legally this was statutory rape. The sex sounded consensual to me, but if the girl is younger than the legal age of consent, it's technically child molestation, rape.

That defined boy friend Waldo as a sexual predator.

There was a link to a newspaper story on the case. The judge had issued a restraining order, and gave the boy a stretch in juvie until he turned eighteen. That was the end of his football career and maybe any chance of a college athletic scholarship. He could be released then, but he was on the books as a sexual offender. Even if the court expunged the record, it was too late. Once your name is out there Google will find it. Talk about a short cut to a ruined life.

Someone had leaked the name of the girl, which should not have happened. She was then bullied on Facebook as a whore. Those high school kids can be vicious, and Tweets tend to be blunt. Words do hurt.

I'm glad they didn't have Twitter when I was in school. I could imagine how awful it would be if someone picked on me. It's bad enough if I have a bad hair day without being taunted about it.

Watching that story unfold I shook my head. Why do kids get themselves in such trouble? I guess it's because of raging hormones and brains not developed enough to sense that there are consequences. The consequences are the worst of it.

Having got all that hate mail, I could relate to the kid. I got sick to my stomach when I learned that the girl had been so badly bullied on Facebook and Twitter she killed herself by jumping off a bridge. When that story got out, the boy friend was overwhelmed with remorse and hanged himself: two deaths because of a teen-aged indiscretion. What a waste. The parents must be heart broken.

The StopRape site had turned into a whirlwind. It wasn't just a place to vent the rage and frustration of rape victims. It also had consequences. Everything has consequences. Unintended consequences like the death of bald eagles when the intention of DDT was to kill mosquitoes is just one example. The reporting of alleged crimes precipitated tragedies. I guess that's why Queen Annie is so careful.

The StopRape.com web site attracted the attention of the *New York Times* and *Time Magazine*. Both were more tenacious than G. Marshall in tracking down the elusive "Maggie" but gave the same excuse that she didn't respond to their attempts at contact. The reporters used the typical dodges like "it is unclear" or "did not respond to our calls," when the truth was they did not know.

Letters to the newspaper editors ranged from support for women's rights to special pleading for the privacy rights of alleged offenders who have never been convicted, not to mention even tried.

Maggie, or whatever her real name was, had stirred the basic emotions of outraged women. I started a scrap book of clippings, screen dumps, and downloaded printouts which I backed up on my 32 gig flash drive. I began to imagine a book about this, a New York contract, a step up from bear stories on WMUP. After all, I had been the first person to interview Maggie. For what that was worth, it made me an insider.

But there was a backlash, law suits for libel. Those were countered by an appeal for the StopRape legal defense fund, to be donated in Bitcoins, that new Internet currency that couldn't be traced. The story was getting really hot.

It had to be more than a one woman show. With all that activity, there had to be a staff handling all the action, like the dot com startup that begins in a garage and grows into something like Facebook. StopRape was a social network and it was getting world wide attention.

I wondered if Maggie had anticipated that kind of reaction. Revenge is a strong motivator, but once Sauvenier, for instance, had his castration, maybe that was enough and it would stop. These things, like rumors, take on a life of their own. They can spiral out of control.

I saw that the web site had a link for instructions, like terrorists have their bomb making sites. There's a point where providing such information is a red flag for law enforcement. For instance, StopRape had an outline plan for how to get away after a physical assault on a rapist. As my Deputy pal Charlie can tell you, it's easy to rob a bank. Getting away with it is something else. He says the Mossad has to train their assassins in the art of escaping, not leaving clues behind, and not getting caught. The killing part is easy.

At what point did providing information become "aiding and abetting"?

As Queen Annie warned me, Maggie of StopRape.com had triggered a viral crime wave.

If it were just the once instance, like the band of sisters that emasculated Sauvenier, the crime might be relatively easy to solve. Usually someone talks, sooner or later. Now there were more cases, cases all over the country. If the purpose of StopRape was to put the fear of God in the minds of the guilty, or the mere suspects, it worked. Frightened men who claimed their sexual encounter was consensual were speaking up at the web site, protesting, demanding that their pictures, names, and addresses be taken down. They were fearful that what happened to Sauvenier could happen to them.

They had reason to be terrified, for anybody whose picture showed up on the web site was fair game. One after another, pictures showed up with a banner slapped across the face, "Castrated." It was as if there were bands of trophy hunters roaming the country and they had knives. Who knew who would be next?

One abused wife had cut off her husband's penis and fed it to their dog. She appeared before a female judge, but if she thought that would get her a more lenient sentence, she was mistaken. She got hard time in the slammer. If the husband had died from loss of blood or an infection it would have been murder, not merely assault to do grievous bodily harm.

Recalling his job as a corrections officer, Charlie says that in prison rapists have high status and pedophiles get murdered. In a woman's prison that penis cutting lady might be high status.

The video of my interview with Maggie on WMUP was viral. Over a million had seen it. It was followed up with clippings of stories of men who had been attacked. My problem was that mine was the only face that showed on the video. Everyone who saw it knew who Kerstin Mikkola was. By association and false logic, some watchers assumed that I was the owner of the web site, not the woman who hid behind the pseudonym Maggie.

Chapter Seven: My Turn in the Barrel

Getting the address of the WMUP TV station was easy, two clicks on Google. At first the mail was addressed to Kerstin Mikkola at WMUP. The simplest message, which required no explanation, was one word: BITCH. The most elaborate was a "cease and desist" lawyer letter complete with an imposing logo and a list of lawyers' names. I was to stop posting faces and names on the StopRape.com site at once or there would be legal action.

Scared, I took the lawyer letter to Queen Annie.

Annie lit a fresh tiny cigar, blew smoke out of the corner of her mouth, and pondered. "You haven't done anything, have you? I mean, besides the interview?"

"I posted a couple of chat room comments, but I didn't mention anyone's name."

Annie shook her head. Her grey hair was pulled back in a bun, making her look older than she is. "You shouldn't have given that woman a copy of the interview."

"I didn't think it would do any harm. It was just for the record."

Annie nodded. "Fair enough. But the broadcast itself belongs to WMUP. It's copyright material. She wasn't authorized to use it for her U-Tube video."

I saw that I had a way out. "U-Tube probably has a contract that nobody can post musical tracks or pictures unless they have legal ownership rights. Maybe I can demand U-tube take down the video."

"Do that right away," Annie advised. "Better draw up a lawyer letter and send it registered mail, return receipt requested."

"I don't have a lawyer," I said, and imagined billable hours piling up against my meager balance at the Savings and Loan.

"The station has liability insurance and libel insurance," Annie said. "The video you passed on to this Maggie person is our property."

"And my face is my property," I added, remembering how a professional footballer had sued when his face was put into an X-box game.

"Don't be so confident, Kerstin. It's a grey area," Annie explained. "You've become news yourself. You are a public figure. When you're a public figure you lose a lot of privacy rights."

"I'll send those lawyers a disclaimer letter."

"Right. And if you're really clever, which I think you are, you can enlist those same lawyers in your suit against StopRape.com for using your face without permission."

I protested. "I can't afford a lawyer."

"If they smell money they'll take your case on speculation. They get 40% of the settlement if you win."

I was reminded of the StopRape legal defense fund. How many bitcoins had Maggie collected? "I'll get on it right away."

"Don't forget, you and Eino are covering a playoff game tonight."

Right. Nothing comes before sports at WMUP. There are overlapping seasons, always some team sport, and in winter snowmobiling and cross country skiing.

What I hate is doing an ice fishing story. I'm always cold. To me there's nothing quite as boring as some Yoopers sitting in a dark ice fishing shelter, staring down into a hole in the lake and waiting for something to bite. This does not make for good TV.

When I showed the hate mail to Charlie he said, "Bitch? And I thought you were a nice girl." He grinned to show he was kidding but I wasn't so sure.

We were eating pizza and drinking beer in my living room on the couch I inherited from my folks when they redecorated. "Maybe I'm a bitch in training," I said.

"You don't have to advertise it," Charlie said. He was still in his deputy uniform though he had left his utility belt and pet Glock behind.

"What do you mean?"

"Didn't you notice?"

He had me. "Notice what?"

"Come on outside," he said.

Puzzled, I slipped on my boots and my storm jacket, the one with the snorkel hood, and we stepped out into the snow. It was still early in the winter and there weren't high snow banks yet, but it was cold even by UP standards. The chill hit me right away. I hadn't brought my gloves and jammed my hands deep into the pockets.

Charlie led me around to the back of my old Taurus and pointed to the bumper.

My heart skipped a beat and I had to catch my breath. I was hit by outrage, shock, and fear all at once. Someone had slapped on a bumper sticker. BITCH.

Whoever did it not only knew where I worked, but where I live, and what I drive. I was beginning to feel like one of those men tagged as a rapist. This was definitely not funny. "You think I'm being stalked?"

"Not necessarily."

I tried to peel off the BITCH sticker, but it was too cold. How was I supposed to get the sticker off? Pour boiling water on it? It was cold enough for snow to squeak under my boots. Maybe anti-freeze would loosen the sticker. Getting it off when it was below zero was going to be, well, a bitch. Some sort of solvent might work, but not to light it or I might incinerate the car. My fingers were already freezing. We went back indoors.

Now I knew how one of the alleged rapists must feel when he's tagged. Not funny. I would have to get that label removed or at least covered up. I'd wanted to slap on a green "Say yah to the UP, hey" bumper sticker. This was probably the time. Might not stick until the temperature got above forty degrees. When would that be? Next March? I didn't have a heated garage, in fact, no garage at all.

I didn't know what else I might do. Sometimes the best defense is to do nothing, not get into a rising argument like someone who takes offense over a remark about the Packers in a bar on Saturday night and ends up knifed in the parking lot.

From then on I paid attention. This StopRape thing wasn't just a curiosity to watch on cyberspace. If I had a stalker, I'd be careful. This was a nice recipe for paranoia.

Chapter Eight: Guns

I followed Queen Annie's advice and wrote the letter to the lawyers. I also put together a stern request to the web site owner not to use my picture, that the interview I had provided was copyright material. I also contacted U-Tube and demanded the video be taken down. So far, so good.

Giga Alert notified me that I was mentioned in other places. The service is free for one notification at a time, but if you want deeper research, they expect some cash. I kicked in twenty bucks and discovered that Kerstin Mikkola was the subject of a lot of chatter, not to mention other Mikkolas, all swept up by the Giga search engine.

At least, knowing who mentioned me and in what context, I could attempt to contact the source and file a disclaimer. I was not part of any plot to emasculate alleged rapists. I had nothing to do with any actions perpetrated by subscribers to the StopRape site.

I had merely interviewed the anonymous woman who set the whole thing up. That should be harmless. I wasn't a co-conspirator.

It's hard. It's like stopping identity theft. They knew my address and there's a ton of stuff about me. If you're trying to get established in the entertainment industry, in television, you want a high profile. If you're the product, you have to publicize yourself. Except I was getting the wrong kind of publicity.

It didn't calm my nerves any when Charlie offered to lend me one of his guns for protection. He said he'd take me to the range to learn how to shoot. He told me I should have a carry permit.

I had no idea that my Charlie Johnson was a gun nut. He lives in an old house he inherited from his mother. It's been insulated and has relatively new siding, but still has the old storm windows which stay on all year and porch steps that sag. He's afraid if he replaces one tread the whole porch will have to come off. But there's nothing dilapidated about his gun safe.

Charlie has what is probably the basic U.P arsenal, a 30-30 hunting rifle with a scope for deer and bear, and a double barreled shotgun for ducks. But he also has one of those Bushmaster assault rifle look-alikes favored by mass shooters. Then there's a couple of hand guns besides the Glock he carries on the job. Somewhere he picked up a World War II souvenir German Luger, possibly from his grandfather. Then there's his thirty-eight caliber Smith & Wesson Police Special.

"This used to be standard issue," Charlie explained as he lovingly held the weapon. It was carefully kept, clean, and he showed me that it was not loaded. "It holds only six shots, so doesn't have the firepower we need nowadays. The magazine for my Glock holds eleven, and you can pop in another in about two seconds." He showed me that you could carry a spare cylinder for the Smith & Wesson.

He showed me how to flip the cylinder to the side and inspect it to see if there were cartridges in it, then handed it to me carefully. He cautioned. "Treat every gun as if it were loaded."

Hefting it, I protested, "It's heavy." I couldn't imagine carrying that thing in my shoulder bag. If I wore it in a holster at my waist I was afraid it would throw my back out. Maybe that's why people who carry weapons walk so funny. It's not the macho swagger. It's the weight. "Don't you have something lighter?"

Charlie had just got a haircut and his buzz cut revealed a sign of early baldness. He scratched the back of his neck, took a deep breath, and explained. "In the movies people hit by one shot go down like a felled tree. Doesn't happen. Might take six or seven to bring someone down."

I thought about that. I remembered that case where a shooter went into a Sikh Temple and killed all those people. He shot a policeman about seven times, but the man was still able to fire back and survived.

I returned the Smith & Wesson. "I don't want to carry that thing around."

Charlie smiled condescendingly. "You want a little pearl handled two shot Derringer you can hide in your muff?"

Not being a follower of old time women's apparel, I wasn't sure what a muff was. Sounded intimate, like underwear. Was he being rude?

Charlie saw that I hadn't understood. He suggested, "We can go to a gun store and find you something lighter and not too expensive."

I had no idea what guns cost. Charlie might lend me his . 38, but I didn't think he was going to actually buy me a woman's gun. "Only if you think it's absolutely necessary." I realized it was almost an agreement.

I appreciated Charlie's concern for my safety, but I thought carrying a gun because of a bumper sticker was overreacting. I could be wrong, but I wasn't ready to start packing heat or whatever they call it down in Detroit. This is the UP, not the big city. We don't have gangs. We do have bears, and all they want is your garbage, not your purse.

If I met a five hundred pound bear in my kitchen and shot it with a pistol all that would do was make it mad.

For the time being, I'd wait on the gun thing.

Chapter Nine: A Victim

I was afraid Eino would notice the BITCH bumper sticker on my Taurus, but if he did he didn't say anything. We used the station's all wheel drive van to hurry out on US41 to get footage of someone who had an argument with a snow plow. The plow won, but by the time we got there the loser was being towed away. The ambulance had already left.

Back at the studio there was someone waiting to see me. She was a girl in her twenties who might have been in an accident herself. She had a black eye, a bruise on her cheek, and strips of stick-on tape to close a cut on her forehead.

I took off my storm coat and hung it on the back of my swivel chair. Still thinking about the snow plow accident I asked, "Were you the driver?"

"What?"

"Sorry, I just came from a highway accident. What happened to you?"

She looked around and lowered her voice. "I was… raped." She had trouble saying the word out aloud.

Eino was hovering and I waved him off.

I lowered my voice. "You should be talking to the police, not to me."

"But you were the one on that TV interview about StopRape."

Just because I do interviews on stories doesn't mean I know everything about them. I'm no authority on rape. Someone told me once that a scientist learns more and more about less and less until he knows everything about nothing, and a journalist learns about more and more until he knows nothing about everything. It's true that I pick up tidbits of information, but there's no depth.

I admit that, thanks to my checking on the StopRape web site and the community of wronged women, I've been paying close attention to the whole rape business but I have no official capacity of any kind. "I just did the interview, hey. I'm not the police and I'm not part of dial HELP. So why come to me?"

She sat on a chair beside my desk, her head down like she was ashamed to look at me. She was obviously traumatized and not being very rational or even coherent. I got a legal pad ready and started asking her questions, simple, basic stuff to calm her down until I got to the heavy stuff.

She said her name was Heather Rasmussen, gave me her address, age twenty-two. The man who attacked her was her boy friend, Joe Pascoe.

I could see already that this was one of those cases that wouldn't survive a cross examination, like yes, she had sex before with the guy, that he liked rough sex, but it was getting out of hand. When she said she had enough and he should stop he got angry and beat her up. The more she protested, the better he liked it. Maybe he thought it was part of the act, but it wasn't.

I guess some people like to be dominated. There are women who want to be a dominatrix complete with handcuffs and whips, but that's not my style or my interest, too kinky for me, and obviously beyond Heather Rasmussen's limits. But this time that limit had been passed. She was injured. She was more than injured. She was violated.

I pointed to the bandage on her forehead. "Who fixed you up?"

"He took me to Marquette General hospital," she said. "Just dumped me at the entrance to the emergency room. Told me to piss off and left."

"Did you tell them at the hospital that you were raped?"

She was ashamed to say and told them she fell down the stairs.

I recognized the battered wife syndrome. Guy beats up wife, then apologizes afterwards, professing undying love— until the next time. I took notes, all the while wondering what she should do next. "Then you didn't get an examination for rape. No vaginal swabs for semen?" Even if the guy wore a condom a real examination might find some of his pubic hairs.

She hadn't been examined.

Not that it would do any good in this circumstance. He was supposedly her boyfriend. They had a history. No rape charge would stick. What alternatives did she have? "You need to go to the police and ask for a restraining order."

Heather didn't know what a restraining order was.

That much I did know. "It means he can't come in contact with you at all or he'll go to jail."

"Can you help me with that?"

"I can't," I admitted. "Maybe I should talk to my boss. Wait here."

I waited just inside the door to Queen Annie's office. She was on the phone with someone at the cable company. She is not great friends with the cable people and I'm not, either, because they keep raising their rates and offering fewer services in their so-called package deals. When she hung up and we made eye contact, I said, "I've got a rape victim here who needs some advice."

She protested, "You know I don't want to run any rape stories."

"I know. Maybe you can advise her about a restraining order. Her name is Heather Rasmussen. Boy friend beat her up."

"Rasmussen. Name sounds familiar." Queen Annie got up from her hair and walked to her glass wall to have a look. "That her?"

"Yep."

"Kids," Annie said, shaking her head as if a one word category was enough. "How old is she?"

"Twenty-two."

"Local?"

"Yooper. She's at the college."

Annie returned to her desk. "Tell you what, Kerstin. I'll call downtown to tell them you're coming and you go along with her to the court house to help her fill out the papers for a restraining order. Might be useful for you to know how this works. Make sure she doesn't back down."

I didn't really want to get involved. It wasn't like Heather Rasmussen was under age and had been a virgin. I knew women could be raped by their husbands who claimed the marriage contract gave them conjugal rights, but Heather wasn't married.

Harley l. Sachs

I explained the situation to her. We'd go to the court and start legal action. She knew where the court house was. I rode along with her to make sure she went. She had an old beater Ford pickup with fenders so rusty they looked like lace, but it ran and, thank goodness, the heater worked.

On the way I suggested she put the boy friend's picture up on the StopRape.com web site along with her story of what he did. I explained how she could do it. I didn't know if she would go that far, but at least she knew how to go about it. Asking for a restraining order kept the case between her, the court, and Pascoe. She had his photograph, but broadcasting his picture on the World Wide Web was a public denunciation. He would not be an anonymous nasty person.

Being in on one of the rapist stories from the beginning would be a good case study for me. That was the journalist in me being cynical and taking advantage.

We don't always do things just out of the goodness of our hearts. We have many reasons for what we do, and helping Heather Rasmussen was only one of them. Getting the story was, to me, at least as important, maybe more so.

Chapter Ten: Restraining

I guided Heather Rasmussen up to the office where she could fill out the papers, but I hung back. I was only there to observe and provide moral support.

She had to fill out a form and describe the reason for her request for a restraining order. Of course, she had to put down the details. It would help if she provided a copy of her hospital bill describing the injuries. This is where she almost got cold feet. She turned to me with a pained look and asked if she had to describe the rape in specific, gory details. I was glad she didn't. It might be good post trauma therapy for her to talk about it, but I didn't need to endure a mental reenactment.

Her attacker was Joe Pascoe, age twenty-four.

I made a note of that for my own purposes. Queen Annie might not want to run a rape story on WMUP television, but as background this could turn into an article for a newspaper or a magazine. If I were a dial HELP counselor or a medical professional I'd be bound by ethics not to reveal any of this, but she came to me as a journalist and I love a good story. Queen Annie might not want to use it, but she doesn't own me. There's nothing in my contract that says I can't write for a print medium. I didn't promise Heather that her story was off the record.

It also doesn't hurt if a story I do on my own can be turned into cash. I was reminded that Charlie advised me to buy a gun, and I didn't know how much they cost.

The clerk who took Miss Rasmussen's report said there'd have to be a hearing. Joe Pascoe might be told to be at the hearing but didn't have to be present. If the application was approved, Pascoe would be served with the court order.

The further this went, the more nervous Heather Rasmussen got. She was, believe it or not, afraid she would get her boy friend in trouble. I assured her that he was in trouble already for assaulting her. If she didn't stop him, he might go on and rape someone else. Sometimes a good punch in the nose like a restraining order would get his attention and he'd wise up. Maybe.

Pascoe wasn't twenty-five yet, the age when men finally figure out that you don't do dumb things like playing chicken on the highway, or raping your girl friend.

On the other hand, I'd read enough stories about men who disobey a restraining order and simply kill the girl friend or wife. The paper a restraining order was printed on was not bullet proof.

Heather drove me back to the television station and I told her to keep in touch. If her boy friend had a key to her place, she should change the lock right away. If she didn't know how to do that herself, I volunteered my friend Charlie to install it if she bought the lock set herself. She should call me as soon as she bought it.

I told Charlie about the case. I'd actually forgotten that changing someone's lock was a service the sheriff's department did for people who were in danger. This was usually some granny whose nephew or grandson was abusing the elderly. It was one of those public safety services most people were unaware of. Did I also know that the fire department would install a smoke alarm? I didn't.

It was like preventive medicine. Being proactive could save people's lives.

When she phoned, I rode with Charlie in a sheriff's patrol car to Heather's apartment. It turned out to be in what had been a duplex provided for military families until the old K.I. Sawyer nuclear war air base was closed. An attempt had been made to refurbish the otherwise abandoned buildings. There was little indication that there had been a community there. The PX and the branch bank office were closed. Nobody had been persuaded to open a grocery store in that location. There wasn't enough traffic. Old military bases can be pretty bleak.

Now commercial flights used the airfield which was how WMUP got the old airport terminal and I got an apartment at the old motel a mile away.

Charlie was familiar with the airbase location, as there had been some incidents there from time to time. K.I. Sawyer wasn't in the city, so it was under the county sheriff's jurisdiction.

Since this was technically county business, we rode out in the patrol car, a Crown Victoria complete with Rhino bars. I hadn't done a ride along with Charlie before. I was squeezed in the front seat beside the GPS, the on board computer, and a shot gun. I realized now what it meant to be "riding shotgun."

Not to block her driveway, he parked the patrol car out in front the house next door to Heather Rasmussen's place. Those military base buildings weren't built to U.P. standards. The front door opened directly into the house, no vestibule for parking boots and snow shoes and keeping out the cold. Heather stood shivering by the open front door.

The old lock was one of those simple things that can be opened with a credit card. Charlie removed it. Heather had gone to a big box store for the lock set and been sold a dead bolt. Charlie had brought his tool box. The installation was a bigger job than just replacing the lock cylinder. Fortunately he has a battery powered portable electric drill.

While we were there a pickup truck drove up. You can tell a lot about a man by what he drives. The truck was one of those with extra big wheels. You would practically need a ladder to climb into the cab. It was one of those macho four wheel drive monsters used for driving in mud races. In spite of it being winter it still sported a coating of died mud that hadn't been washed off.

A man got out. He was tall, skinny, with high cheekbones and an affected beard under his lower lip. He was wearing work boots, faded jeans with torn knees, a jacket that looked like it had been worn under a car while he'd been changing the oil, and a look of suspicion and anger.

I guessed it was Pascoe, the offending boy friend, and I was right. He'd noticed the sheriff's car, but it was parked outside the next house. "What's this?" he asked.

Charlie was hunched over the new lock in his heavy uniform jacket, so until he turned around you didn't see his deputy badge. He had tightened the last screw and was testing the new key. When he turned around the visitor backed up a couple of feet.

I asked, "Are you Joe Pascoe?"

46

He was surprised. "Yeh. Who are you?"

I looked him in the eye. "Kerstin Mikkola, WMUP. I'm doing a story about a rape." That wasn't exactly true, of course, since Queen Annie wouldn't do a rape story, but there were other possible places to sell the story.

Pascoe took in the sight of the patrol car, the uniformed deputy at the door. At first he pretended ignorance. "Rape? What rape?"

"Heather Rasmussen."

Pascoe avoided my look. "Bullshit. That wasn't rape."

Charlie had finished the job. He handed the pair of keys through the partly opened door where a frightened Heather Rasmussen took them. The door slammed shut and the lock clicked.

Charlie shut his tool box and stood up, a picture of stern authority. "If you're Joe Pascoe, you'll be served with a restraining order. That means you're not to have any contact with Miss Rasmussen. No phone calls, no letters, no visits, no harassment. If you violate the order you'll be arrested and jailed for contempt of court."

Pascoe looked like he might, under other circumstances, throw a punch. He shouted at the closed door, "Heather! What the fuck is this?"

"You'd better just leave," Charlie said. "Now."

We waited until he drove off, those big tires spinning in the snow.

Charlie advised, "You didn't have to tell him your name."

I admitted, "I was trying to intimidate him by mentioning the TV station."

"Some people aren't intimidated. They look at things as if they are a challenge. I think we'd better see if this Joe Pascoe has a rap sheet."

Chapter Eleven: Pascoe Posted

Charlie dropped me off at the TV station. I didn't have time to research Joe Pascoe's record, if he had one, because we had the six o'clock news coming up. Queen Annie, always the sports fan, wanted to know if we'd have time to do a quick interview with the university's ice hockey coach? There wasn't time for me and Eino to get to the rink, do a quick taping, and get back to edit it.

Fortunately, the ice hockey coach was so hungry for publicity that he rushed to the studio. He showed up appropriately dressed in a brightly colored team jacket. I was afraid the color clash would cause problems for Eino who was operating the studio camera. It's best to wear muted, solid colors for a broadcast, not, for example, something with small checks. I never wear a white blouse, either, but something pale blue to avoid flares. Fortunately, the team jacket seemed to work.

It's a stressful job, always being on deadline. WMUP is not a big station and the crew is basic. There was a quick edit, piecing together the news clips, then the broadcast. Just to add to my tension, Sarah, the girl who regularly does the weather report was off sick and I had to fill in, not my strong point. I'm not into isobars and my idea of UP weather is one word: snow.

At least I don't work the control room with the monitors and switching, keeping the commercials queued up, and not going to black. It's not the kind of job that allows for a potty break.

I didn't have a moment to spare for Joe Pascoe until after the show. I sat down at my monitor, took a deep breath, and Googled him. It turned out there were literally hundreds of Pascoe hits, including a British mystery TV series. It was a case of too much information. The best place to hide a needle wasn't in a haystack but in a needle factory. Which needle? Which Pascoe?

Pascoe was an unusual name, but, using the right key words for the search, I finally thought I had it narrowed down. The white pages yielded Joe Pascoes in what looked like an extended family. Was he Joe Junior? Even then, getting a complete police record wasn't free. I didn't want to pay the required fee so I called Charlie. He was out on patrol. I talked to him on the car radio and he promised to come by my place after work for a bribe of chili and corn bread to do a computer search for Joe Pascoe's police record, if any. As a deputy he had access.

That was the neat thing about the Internet. If you had the right passwords and protocol you could find out anything. It wasn't like the graduate school research I did B.C., before computers, when you did frustrating searches in the library stacks only to find out that the page you wanted had been torn out by someone too lazy to take notes or too cheap to pay for a photo copy.

When Charlie showed up he'd had a shower and smelled of after shave, so I was sure he had other things in mind besides chili and corn bread. I popped the tabs on a couple of Buds and kept the conversation on the rape case. Finally, with some reluctance, he sat down at my laptop to find out the details on Joe Pascoe.

It didn't take him long. Charlie shook his head and sighed. "Look at this, Kerstin. He's had a couple of drunk driving tickets, with points on his license. He was arrested for assault outside a bar, suspended sentence. This guys a bad ass."

I supposed that if I got a parking ticket in Detroit and didn't pay it, it would pursue me and show up when I tried to renew my driver's license.

But there was more about Pascoe. "It gets worse," Charlie continued. "At a traffic stop his truck was searched and they found a stolen rifle behind the seat."

"Stolen?"

Charlie sniffed. "Old story. He claimed he bought it from someone. No proof, but the weapon was confiscated and returned to the owner, who turned out to be someone from Wisconsin who'd had the rifle in his hunting camp near

Crystal Falls." Burglarizing cabins in the off season is fairly common. When people return for their summer vacations they sometimes discover that all their stuff has been stolen, furniture and all. Granny's antique rocking chair might show up at a flea market in Minnesota.

Joe Pascoe sounded to me like a mean drunk who would eventually end up in jail.

Charlie shut down the computer. "That's it. You might want to warn Heather Rasmussen about his record. Pascoe is bad news."

I agreed. I wondered how a girl like Heather Rasmussen would hook up with someone like Pascoe. Maybe he had charm. Not my type of charm, of course.

Maybe she wasn't such a nice girl herself.

Charlie turned in my cheapie office chair and grinned at me as he shut down the computer. "Now let's get to something more fun." He expected more than chili and corn bread.

I was game. At least this time his pager didn't go off while we were in bed.

Charlie didn't stay the night, and after he left I was still distracted by the Rasmussen situation. I wondered if Heather had followed through and posted Pascoe's picture and her story on the StopRape.com web site.

I guess she was over her worry that she might get him in trouble with the restraining order. Her trauma and self-guilt for having engaged in rough sex with Pascoe had evolved into anger. By golly, you betcha, there it was, Joe Pascoe, accused rapist, posted at StopRape with the story. Heather, following the protocol, had used a screen name, not her real identity, but if Pascoe saw it he'd have no doubt who posted it.

I assumed Heather Rasmussen would have a supply of RAPIST bumper stickers, but I wouldn't advise her to slap one on the back of Pascoe's mud truck. You don't irritate a rattle snake. You might get bitten.

Chapter Twelve: Guns

It didn't take more than a couple of days before I saw that filthy pickup truck parked outside the TV station when I arrived for work. Pascoe was waiting for me. The dirty jacket was familiar.

He's a scary guy, tall, unshaven and smelly. He blocked my entrance to the KBUP building and waved a paper in my face. He was obviously steaming mad. "You put her up to this."

I feigned ignorance. "Put who up to what?"

He held it up to my face. "It's a restraining order."

I hadn't actually seen one before, but he pulled it away before I got a chance to read more than a couple of lines. "I guess that means you can't see her."

"You stay out of my business," Pascoe warned.

"I'm not in your business."

"Just watch your back, bitch."

Maybe he'd seen the sticker on the bumper of my Taurus. I hadn't managed to get it off. It was too cold. "Don't worry. You aren't going to be on TV. I hope you're not disappointed."

"Maybe not TV, but I got a call from a buddy who said my face is on a web site called StopRape."

"Oh." I pretended not to have seen it. "Your picture is on the Internet?" I forced a smile. "You'll be famous."

"Don't make fun of me, bitch. It ain't funny."

"Rape isn't funny."

"It wasn't rape."

I had to cut this off. "Look, I'm sorry you got yourself into so much trouble. Now I have to go to work, if you don't mind."

I got past him and he shouted after me, "I'm gonna get a lawyer and sue you for declaration!"

I corrected him. "You mean defamation."

"Whatever."

That was plain silly. I'd never mentioned him on the air. I wasn't spreading rumors about him. So far as I could see, the only lawyer Joe Pascoe would ever get was a public defender who would persuade him to plead guilty.

But when I saw him slip while trying to climb into that awful truck I had a twinge of pity for the guy. It takes two to tango, and Heather Rasmussen had to bear some responsibility for their relationship. Early on she could have said simply, "No."

The encounter with Pascoe and his threat convinced me that Charlie had a point about the gun thing. Next time I saw him I told him I'd take him up on that offer to take me to the shooting range.

Not that I was interested in that .38 caliber Smith & Wesson police cannon. I didn't feel comfortable with the idea of packing heat like some Detroit hood, but it might be useful to be at least familiar with firearms. A journalist needs to know something about everything and knowing how to shoot might be helpful.

Morning was the best time for my schedule, so we made a date.

The local sportsman's club is in an old log cabin lodge about five miles out of town. The driveway back to it was actually plowed, even though I was sure it's not a county road. Somebody with a blade on a four wheel drive truck could clear it, or maybe someone had a friend on the highway crew who made a brief detour into the woods.

There was no wind and the smoke from the stone chimney went straight up. There was someone there, an old guy Charlie knew by his appropriate nickname, Smokey, a man with a full beard going grey and, I discovered, a gamey leg. He wore a vet's jacket with Vietnam shoulder patches and smelled of wood smoke.

The wood stove was hot, but the room was still chilled. There were antlers mounted on the walls and a big, dusty, moth-eaten, stuffed moose head.

We don't hunt moose here, though they've been reintroduced in spite of the risk of brain worm. I once did an interview on that or I'd think brain worm was like a computer virus. Even without moose or elk, the UP is a hunter's paradise. There are bears, deer, small game, rabbits, ducks, geese, and partridge in season. If not shooting something, there was always fishing, summer and winter. If you look at the calendar there are only a couple of weeks in the entire year when something isn't in season. That's when Yoopers stay home to clean their guns, oil the reels, tie some flies, and make plans for the next round.

I'm not into any of it. I don't have any hobbies, and I'm not into crafts like knitting scarves or sweaters. I'll save that for my old age. I suppose you could call me a workaholic, because if I'm not busy at WMUP I'm watching the competition on TV at home, taking notes, and thinking what I might do if I had my own show.

Anyway, I found myself bundled up to the eyes against the cold while Charlie guided me out though shin deep snow to the sportsman's club shooting range behind the lodge. We had to brush the latest snow off the counter where Charlie carefully laid out the weapons he would show me.

He walked me through the drill on how to behave around any firearm. For one, you always assumed it was loaded and you never pointed it at anybody unless you were prepared to shoot them. I wasn't dumb enough to look down the barrel to see how the bullet came out when I pulled the trigger. I heard some idiots did, but never more than once.

We tried several weapons. I even tried Charlie's Glock and was impressed. My God, you could fire ten shots in less than ten seconds. No wonder the old Smith & Wesson revolver was for collectors and museums.

Charlie showed me a shooting stance, holding the gun with both hands to steady it against the recoil. What also intimidated me was the noise. It was like a cannon going off in your ear. I just didn't think it was fun.

I was also a lousy shot. Even braced, I couldn't hold a hand gun steady. The Sportsman's Club had some targets set out for various distances, and it was a miracle if I hit them at all.

Finally, in frustration, Charlie suggested that if I was afraid of home invasion I should have a .410 coachman shotgun. It has the shortest legal barrel, and unlike a 9 mm bullet, it couldn't penetrate the walls and kill someone in their bed half a block away. But a shotgun didn't require dead eye aim in order to intimidate somebody.

A .410 could kill rabbits. What would I do with a rabbit if I did shoot it? I didn't want to kill anything or anybody.

I didn't know anything about shotguns and Charlie hadn't brought one along. He explained that they didn't fire bullets, just pellets like a BB gun, but a bunch of them that spread out so you didn't have to have perfect aim.

We'd go to a gun store and see if we could find one.

We said goodbye to Smokey, the old Viet vet. On the way back to town Charlie tried to explain to me the difference between a twelve gauge and the .410, different kinds of shot. Lead shot had been made illegal because lead shot on the bottom of a duck pond got eaten by the ducks who then died of lead poisoning. Steel shot didn't have the same punch, but didn't poison the environment.

All that went right by me. I wasn't going duck hunting and with luck even if I had a shotgun for home protection, I hoped not to ever use it. The more I thought about it, the more nervous I got. The whole business of guns freaked me out. Now I felt compelled go to along with the idea.

Since I wasn't interested in a hand gun we ended up at Wal-Mart. It's now a super store, complete with a meat department and frozen foods. I knew that department but had never been at the back where they sell fishing gear and, yes, lots of guns. You could equip half an army there. They had just about everything, even little one shot .22 rifles in pink for, I shuddered at the thought, little girl shooters.

Offering a little, pink single shot .22 made it look like a toy, but it could still kill someone. Why did anyone want their little kid to be capable of killing anybody? When I was a kid we didn't even play cops and robbers with home made rubber band guns. I was living in a gun crazy society.

Until that encounter with Joe Pascoe, I felt safe. A rubber band gun wouldn't protect me from someone like him. Maybe I could use mace or pepper spray. If I didn't have that, how could I defend myself? This was giving me a serious case of paranoia.

The clerk at Wal-Mart didn't have what Charlie recommended, but he could order one for me, a short barrel . 410 preferably with a magazine so it wouldn't have to be reloaded after every shot.

I was relieved that they didn't have one in stock. I could postpone the whole business, not think about it. I didn't want to think about owning a shotgun, like where to keep it, loaded or unloaded. Beside my bed? Under it? A shotgun is too big to hide under your pillow. If someone was breaking in, would I have time to find the ammunition and load it? What if this was happening at four in the morning when I was mostly asleep? It sounded like the risks of having a firearm were greater than the risks of actual home invasion. Statistically, that was true.

I could imagine that someone with an arsenal in a gun safe might have trouble finding the key in case of an emergency. And if you had kids in the house, curious little boys, how would you be sure they weren't playing quick draw McGraw while you were out shoveling the driveway? So many kids died while playing with guns. To me a firearm was more of a liability.

Back at my computer I checked the StopRape Facebook page and was appalled at the vitriol. There sure were a lot of angry women out there. I wondered how much it would take before it was open season on men, mobs of irate women patrolling the neighborhoods with their own .410 shotguns or worse. Give a rapee an assault rifle, and watch out.

The unemployment figures showed that things were tough on certain age groups of men. American men were an endangered species.

One female commentator said the bees had the right idea. Once the drone male bee mated with the queen, he died. Men were virtually obsolete.

No wonder some men were angry, frustrated, and took it out on their wives and girl friends. It reminded me of Joe Pascoe. He was one of those angry men. Restraining order or not, what would he do?

I searched U-tube and saw that the StopRape video with my interview, my face, and my name, had been taken down and replaced with a new one. It was more graphic and grim, but at least I wasn't associated with it.

I breathed a sigh of relief and thought I was home free on that score. But I was wrong.

Chapter Thirteen: Strange phone calls

I got a long distance phone call at the TV station from a man who said he was working for a newspaper in California. I thought he said the San Diego something, but he said it so fast I didn't catch it.

"I'm calling about the Sauvenier case," he said. "I saw by the comment you posted on the StopRape web site that you know something about it."

Whoops! How did he know it was me? "How did you get my name?"

"Before it was taken down from U-Tube I saw your video interview, and then the comment you made so I put two and two together."

First the hate mail sent to the station, then the BITCH sticker on my bumper. You couldn't hide these days. Nothing was anonymous. So much for privacy. What next? "I know nothing more than I guessed that Sauvenier is the man who raped Maggie, the woman who set up the web site. She's no longer in the military."

"So her name really is Maggie?"

"That's the name she gave us. I don't know her real identity." Nuts. Everyone knew mine, but this Maggie had managed to stay anonymous.

"Do you know where she lives?"

"I'm sure she's not in California. I think she might be in Michigan," I said. "The FBI's looking for her, too. What did you say your name was?"

"Larry Parks."

I didn't believe that for a minute. Why didn't he say his name was Jimmy Stewart? "And the newspaper you're working for?"

He hesitated before answering. "The San Jose Examiner."

This time I wrote it down. It was my turn to ask the questions. "So you think Maggie or whatever her name is was behind the mutilation of Sauvenier?"

"She or someone she organized for revenge."

"Beats me," I said. "All I know is what I got when I interviewed her. I'm in the Upper Peninsula of Michigan, hey. So I take it you think there's some kind of conspiracy?"

The guy who claimed to be Larry Parks said, "I'm just following leads."

"If you find something out, why not let me know? You've obviously got my number."

His answer didn't sound like a promise. End of conversation.

We have caller ID but it said "caller unknown," so I didn't get his number. Then when I Googled the San Diego Examiner I found out there was no such newspaper. So who the hell was Larry Parks and why was he calling me?

Maybe he was really a lawyer for Mrs. Sauvenier planning to sue for loss of service.

I was rattled and distracted. Then I got another call, this time from a woman. "My name is Mary Kimpton," she said. I'm calling for Women Warriors United Against Abuse."

I figured she was going to ask for money. Ready to hang up, I said, "I don't donate to telephone solicitors."

"Money would be appreciated, but I'd like to invite you to our next meeting."

Now I was curious. What were they? Were they a group of concerned citizens like the League of Women Voters, or something sinister, a female secret society, a version of the KKK, except their target was abusers of any color or stripe? My morbid imagination was running wild. For a moment I pictured a vigilante group bent on emasculations. Maybe, like some Vietnam vets who collected human body parts as war souvenirs, there was a gang of tough gals collecting rapists' testicles. It was enough to turn my stomach. "What's your purpose?"

"Broadly speaking, it's a response to the war against women."

That sounded more benign. I wasn't going to commit myself to anything over the phone. "Why don't you send me something in writing about your organization?" I suggested. "Send it to me here at WMUP." Not that I didn't think she'd find out my home address, I just didn't want the world beating a path to my door. I didn't want to be a magnet for everyone with a chip on his shoulder.

Maybe I already was.

The next call actually was to my own phone at home, and it was past midnight. I had been at the station for the ten o'clock news. It was a long day, and I was bushed. My apartment has a tub and shower but the tub won't hold water: I would really enjoy a nice, warm soak. Some day if I own my own house or condo I'll have a hot tub with massaging water jets. Luxury.

The phone was ringing when I got out and was toweling myself off. I padded into the bedroom in towel and bare feet and picked up. "Hello?"

There was someone there, but they didn't say anything. Maybe it's a wrong number, I thought, but they didn't just hang up. It was one of those heavy breathers. Irritated, I hung up. I wondered if the caller was the same one that put the BITCH sticker on my bumper. The caller ID was blocked.

I was beginning to hope that Wal-Mart would call pretty soon to say my shotgun was ready.

An hour later, when I was falling asleep, the phone rang again. This time there was someone there, but all he said was "Bitch" and hung up before I could reply, "Asshole."

This was not funny. I'd have to talk to Queen Annie about it. She knows how to deal with just about anything. Must be the character building effect of those little cigars she smokes.

I didn't sleep well, for I was afraid I'd be called every hour all night. I turned off the ringer of the phone and the answering machine, too, so if there was a call, I wouldn't be disturbed.

The next morning I asked Queen Annie for advice. "I've been getting some strange phone calls," I began.

"Like what?"

"Well, yesterday there was a call from someone who claimed to be a reporter for the San Diego Examiner, except there's no such newspaper. Then I got an invitation to attend a meeting of Women Warriors United Against Abuse. Ever hear of it?"

"Nope. Did you check them out on the Internet?"

I admit, I'd forgotten to do that. "Then I got harassing calls last night. You know, the heavy breathing kind."

Annie drew on her little cigar, saw that it had gone out, and lit it again with that antique Zippo lighter. "For the phone call, you can do a couple of things. Keep a log of the calls, date and time. Then you can make a police report and get the phone company to put a trap on your line."

I'd never head of that. "How's that work?"

"The phone company keeps a record of the calls you get and when you have enough evidence you can have the police step in. Were these threatening calls?"

"Not unless being called a bitch is threatening."

"Then I'd suggest you have the phone company set up a call block. Unless the caller enters a number you specify, they can't get through."

"You mean like 'press one to talk to Kerstin?'"

"Something like that. The only your friends who know the secret number can call you."

That sounded better to me. I'd better call Charlie to tell him about the harassing caller and the secret number.

What I didn't like at all about this business was I was beginning to get a siege mentality. All this because I had interviewed an angry woman for the six o'clock news. Go figure.

Good thing I wasn't harassed if someone didn't like the hockey score. WMUP is on the network cable, and people do call up sometimes if they think the soap opera stinks, as if we had some impact on network content. Maybe those people just don't have anyone else to complain to and call the station. Maybe they're lonely.

I got an image of solitary, insomniac recluses sitting by their televisions needing companionship. It was a good argument to get a dog. A TV may be entertaining, but it is not good company.

Setting up the phone block thing was pretty easy. Then I called Charlie to tell him what was happening. I tried to make it sound like nothing special, but he was worried. He had his reasons. After his couple of years as a corrections officer at the prison he knew there were really bad people out there. They had friends on the outside that owed them favors in payment for protection while inside the prison. Had I offended some prisoner?

I tried to think about that one. I had interviewed a couple of bad characters at one time or another, people who were suing someone or under arrest. It was just routine stuff, hey. Unless they said something incriminating on camera, my interviews had no impact on their convictions.

In my job you see an awful lot of people. Even though the interviews can be preempted by something more important and don't make it to the actual broadcast, for the person involved it's a big deal. I'd get a protest phone call, "Why didn't you run my interview?" At WMUP a five minute interview might end up as thirty seconds or nothing.

I just report the news. I don't create it. Trouble is, there's still a tendency in some circles to blame the messenger. In Roman times, as I learned in journalism school, the bearer of bad news might be killed. I didn't want to be killed because I interviewed the woman called Maggie about her StopRape web site.

Even though I was a subscriber to the web site in order to access the gory details of the exposes, that didn't make me a co-conspirator.

Chapter Fourteen: A visitor

As if all that weren't enough, I got another call from G. Marshall, the FBI guy. This time he made an appointment and he wanted to see me at my home. I guess he sensed that Eino had big ears.

I agreed. I told him I often worked late in the evening, what with the six o'clock and later the ten o'clock news, and sometimes didn't get home until after midnight. Could he stop by in the morning, like eight o'clock? If there was fresh snow, maybe I could talk him into shoveling my front steps, make him earn his government paycheck.

Eight o'clock was OK. I was up at 6:30, tidied up the place, and had a pot of coffee ready, a stained but otherwise clean WMUP mug, and a plate with a few stale peanut butter cookies. I wasn't going to lay on breakfast. I had my own souvenir mug from my days working at the Chinook Winds casino. If he expected more, he could buy me breakfast at a local restaurant.

I wish I had thought of that, because those guys get per diem and he could write it off. But I remembered he didn't want anyone observing us. This is a small town. Everybody knows everybody's business. Thanks to WMUP I'm a public figure. If I showed up at the Mather Inn with a guy in a three piece suit, the word would filter back to Charlie.

Right on time there was a knock at my door. I looked through the peephole Charlie had installed for me months ago. Sure enough. G. Marshall. "Come on in."

He was carrying a thin attaché case and wore a hip length heavy winter jacket with a snorkel hood and waffle stomper boots like some Yooper. Maybe that was his attempt to look local. He surprised me by taking off the boots inside the front door so he wouldn't track snow on the carpet. The guy was polite.

In his heavy wool stocking feet he didn't seem so intimidating, and when he took off his jacket, except for his shoulder holster and gun, he looked like any other civilian in a heavy Norwegian patterned ski sweater.

Not afraid to tease the FBI, I asked, "This your disguise?"

"No. This is me."

He accepted the offer of coffee, no cream or sugar, and even took a bite of one of the cookies before he got down to business. "I see you are a subscriber to the StopRape web site and a regular visitor to the Facebook pages."

"You must have a direct line to the NSA snoops," I said. "What of it? I'm not breaking any laws. I'm just an investigating reporter."

"I thought we might share some information."

I could sense the pitch coming, that he wanted me to be an FBI informant. "Just so I don't break any fourth estate ethics," I cautioned.

"What do you know about Women Warriors United Against Abuse?"

What did I have, a party line? "If you tapped the WMUP phones then you heard my conversation and know as much as I do."

"We're not tapping the WMUP phones," Agent Marshall said, but he averted his eyes and I suspected he was lying.

"Maybe you could tap mine," I suggested. "I've been getting some nasty phone calls, the heavy breathing kind. You could find out whose trying to scare me."

Just saying it made me realize that I was scared. It might be a good thing to have Agent Marshall in my court.

He was interested, but he didn't write anything down, and I wondered if he was wearing a wire and recording everything like I've seen in the movies. The harassing phone calls didn't seem to interest him, but I was willing to bet he'd follow upon my comment. I hoped.

Like a bull dog he stuck to his main purpose. "Have you been in touch with Imogene Michener?"

"Who's that?"

"The woman behind the StopRape web site."

I tried not to drop my casino mug. He knew more than I did, which was appropriate, since he was FBI. So now I knew Maggie's name. "Never heard of her. She told us her name was Maggie."

He unzipped the attaché case and slid out a pixilated, black and white photograph that looked like a bad computer screen dump. "Is this the woman you interviewed?"

I put down my Casino mug and studied the picture. It was printed on ordinary copy paper, which didn't help the clarity any. The hairdo was different. "That could be her. That could be Maggie. Is Michener her real name?"

"Imogene Michener may simply be a stolen identity or an alias," G. Marshall explained. "Have you contacted her?"

I shook my head. I was totally in the dark. "Not directly. There's the Facebook page and the chat rooms. I haven't seen anybody named Imogene. People use screen names."

"They also use code words," Marshall explained. "I think when someone says they're going shopping and looking for a bargain, what they're really saying is they're hunting and the bargain is a potential victim."

It was beginning to sound like the Mafia. I'd heard that when a Mafioso asked for a carpenter he was actually looking for a hit man. "So there are more victims than Sauvenier?"

G. Marshall sighed and put down his mug. "The assault on Master Sergeant Carlos Wayne Sauvenier and the StopRape web page may have set off a string of related attacks on men whose pictures have been posted. What we're trying to find out is if it's just coincidence or if there is a link."

"You mean like if there's a link between school shootings, or just copycats?" I hadn't run into any other cases of emasculations of alleged rapists. I hadn't looked, either. But a nationwide movement? I couldn't believe it.

Women who were raped were often ashamed, didn't want to report it, blamed themselves. Even Heather Rasmussen didn't want to get that jerk Pascoe in trouble. Go figure. I couldn't imagine Heather calling in the troops to take their revenge. I was beginning to think that Agent Marshall was a conspiracy nut.

"Bad ideas take on a life of their own," Marshall said.

"If it's spontaneous, you'd never be able to track them down. I mean, nobody anticipated those school shootings."

Marshall took another cookie. Maybe he hadn't had breakfast after all. "It's not the same thing. There's no web site for wannabe school shooters, and no national association, either."

That got me to thinking.

Imogene Michener might be a wannabe Mullah like those who use the Internet to preach Jihad terrorism to recruit suicide bombers and the like. "I haven't seen anything that you could interpret as recruiting victims for revenge," I said. "Not on the web site, though some of the Facebook comments are pretty angry."

Marshall agreed. He was waiting for me to tell him more.

"Look, Mr. Marshall, at a baseball game you might shout 'kill the umpire,' but nobody goes out and does it. Some woman might say the rapist should have his nuts cut off, but that doesn't mean she'd actually do it."

The plain language seemed to upset him. Marshall set down his WMUP mug and covered his lap with the attaché case as if he might be shielding his own jewels.

He'd had enough. "If you see or hear anything, get in touch with me. You have my card."

Chapter fifteen: .410 lock and load.

I debated about calling Charlie to tell him that G. Marshall had visited. I was about to reach for the phone when it rang. Of course, it was blocked but the caller ID said it was Wal-Mart, so I picked up. It was a robo call, but the message was that my order was ready to be picked up. I had only one order: the shotgun.

Maybe I could run over there during my lunch break.

I'd had to fill out papers for a background check when I placed the order, but that had cleared. I am not a known felon, an escapee from the lunatic asylum, have no restraining order against me, and am not on parole. Those were the same questions I'd have to answer to get a concealed weapon carry permit.

I hadn't taken that step yet, mainly because the brief introduction Charlie had given me on the Sportsman's Club range wasn't enough to qualify me as having passed a firearms course. Anyway, I didn't need a concealed weapon carry permit if all I wanted to buy was an ordinary hunting weapon. I didn't even need a hunting license. All I needed was cash.

For the man at the gun counter the sale was routine, but for me it was a major step to own a real firearm even if it was a mere .410 rabbit gun. At least I wasn't buying a girlie pink single shot .22. Then I'd feel silly.

I got talked into a gun case, a cleaning kit, and a couple of boxes of shells. As I signed the credit card slip I was painfully aware that now Visa knew I had bought a fire arm, and no doubt so did the NSA and G. Marshall. It wasn't only

NSA that was watching. Aggressive marketers were, too, using metadata to push products. I supposed that now I'd get emails from Wal-Mart offering hunting clothes, boots, and a camouflaged duck boat.

Of course, thanks to the credit card receipts and the so-called club card for discounts, the grocery store has a computer record of everything I eat. For all I know I might get a warning from the National Department of Health to cut down on peanut butter cookies. Big brother or big daddy, or big momma was watching.

Eino was watching, too, when I brought my new gun case into the television studio. I didn't dare leave it in the trunk of my Taurus. If someone like Joe Pascoe or some other potential car prowlers had seen me buy it at the Wal-Mart I might have been followed.

Eino recognized the case and asked, "Going hunting?"

All this suspicion and stress was getting to me. "I thought I might go on safari and shoot elephants."

"Elephants are protected."

I struck my forehead in feigned surprise. "You betcha. I shouldn't have fallen for that sales talk."

Eino understood that he wasn't going to worm the truth out of me and let it go.

I called Charlie and told him the .410 had arrived and when was he going to teach me how to use it.

For that we had to wait until Sunday morning. Neither Charlie nor I go to any church, and it looked like half the local hunters don't either, for the Sportsman's Club parking lot had been plowed and was full of beater cars and pickups. The lodge was crowded with mostly men, a few middle-aged women, and dogs. You can't sell alcohol in Michigan before noon on Sunday, but I guessed the rule doesn't apply to private clubs, for there was beer flowing and Smokey was busy pouring behind the bar.

It turned out they were having a Beagle contest to see whose rabbit dog was the best. It was the Yooper version of the British fox hunts, only without horses. At first I thought it would make for a good TV report but I didn't have Eino and his camera along.

While the dog people went out to a course, the actual shooting range wasn't crowded. A couple of guys were sighting in their rifles and one was showing of his Bushmaster assault rifle, quickly emptying a magazine as he fired away at one of the deer-shaped targets. I didn't see how it was very sportsmanlike to use a near machine gun to hunt deer, but what do I know?

I told myself the guy was just showing off, but considering the price of bullets, it was an expensive brag.

By comparison my new .410 was a pea shooter. It might get a rabbit if it wasn't more than maybe fifty feet away, but it wasn't rabbits I needed to protect myself from. If anything, I might—I hoped not—use it against a burglar in my entry way or living room where I couldn't miss. I was gaining confidence.

Charlie warned me, if I had to shoot someone, I could, but if I had time to think about it, I might hesitate too long. It was a dangerous moment to evaluate the situation and make damned sure before pulling the trigger.

He knew. Fortunately, though he was a deputy he had never had to shoot anybody. As a prison guard he had been armed with a uniform and a pencil. Both were successful intimidators, for with a pencil he could write an offender a ticket to loss of commissary privileges or even solitary confinement.

After I'd wasted half a box of shells Charlie showed me how to clean and oil the gun. A rusty weapon was useless.

Trouble was, now that I had a potentially lethal firearm, where would I keep it when I wasn't at home? I didn't have a gun safe like Charlie. It wouldn't do if I came home and found out it had been stolen. I hadn't even paid for it yet.

One step at a time, I told myself. It's like a fire extinguisher. You want to have it and hope never to need to use it.

Chapter sixteen: subpoena

I reflected that my life had changed drastically since that apparently innocent interview with the woman who called herself Maggie. Now I knew, or thought I knew that her real name was Imogene Michener.

The hate mail had tapered off, probably because the U-tube clip with my picture had been taken down. It had become almost routine. I'd open the envelopes, make a copy on WMUP's machine, bundle up the originals and mail them to the StopRape.com post office box in Minneapolis. I was acquiring a little collection of BITCH bumper stickers. Maybe there was a counter web site somewhere to organize the protestors, or a Facebook page with a link to where you could buy the stickers. I hadn't researched that. After all, I have a job to do. I had to concentrate on real drama, like the school bus that got stuck in the snow for two hours and kids getting frost bite. That's life in he UP. But then I got another unexpected visitor.

I saw him out of the corner of my eye when he came in the station door and went directly to Queen Annie's glass office. I saw the pantomime as she nodded and pointed through the window at me.

The man didn't look local. For one, he was wearing dress shoes, not boots, and an overcoat, no hat. He looked pretty young and had curly, black hair and a fresh shave. I don't know if lawyers have a certain look or not, but I pegged him for a recent law school graduate with a gofer job.

I was right. The gofer job was to serve me with a subpoena. It was a folded piece of paper with my name on the front fold: Kerstin Mikkola. I asked, "What's this for? Am I being sued for something?"

I immediately thought of Joe Pascoe. Surely he hadn't actually gone for a lawyer because of that restraining order over Heather.

I guessed that all my visitor had to do was confirm that I was Kerstin Mikkola, hand me the document, then split. Rather reluctantly he explained in words that seemed unfamiliar to him, too. "You're a witness in a class action suit."

"What suit?"

"It's a law suit for defamation by a group of men who have been wrongly identified as rapists on the StopRape.com web site. Since you were in the U-Tube video and are a subscriber, you are a witness."

So they knew I was a subscriber. Maybe I should have tried to be anonymous when I subscribed, used a screen name when I commented at the chat page. I'd let my ego get in the way. Now I was being paid back for my lust for fame.

I remembered the name G. Marshall had given me and the pixilated photograph. "So who's being sued? You can't sue a web site."

"No, but besides the woman who is the owner of the site, there are people working for her, collecting bitcoins for the defense fund, giving legal advice, and instructions on how to get away after mutilating some victim. The class action suit is going after the whole bunch."

What I figured right away was the lawyers were going after billable hours for the bitcoin stash. I saw nothing in my lurking on the site that would indicate actual encouragement of women to attack the alleged rapists. I knew the contract women, and men for that matter, who posted pictures of their attackers, had to sign. They accepted full legal responsibility for the content of what they posted. I didn't think the suit would go anywhere.

My visitor left and I headed directly to Queen Annie's office. She'd been watching the whole time. I showed her the subpoena. "Look at this."

Queen Annie is at the age where she needs reading glasses which she looks over the top of most of the time.

I asked, "Do I have to appear in court? I don't know where this is to take place."

For a moment I had a fantasy about being flown out to San Diego business class at the plaintiffs' expense and put up in a nice hotel near the beach until I had to testify. A case like that could go on for a long time. Might be a great escape from UP snow and cold. What would I wear? Would there be a pool? Better pack a bathing suit.

"You may not be called," Annie said, studying the fine print. "You could probably do a deposition by Skype."

There went that pipe dream.

I figured Queen Annie had all the answers. "So what do I do now?"

"Sit on it. Nothing may come of it." Now she took off those reading glasses and gave me a stern look. "Do your job. Forget this distraction. Just listen to your scanner for police calls worthy of TV coverage."

She had a point, of course. Thank goodness we almost never have a case when some guy takes hostages and barricades himself in his house for hours or days while Eino and I try to keep warm in the TV van. Besides standing around in the snow waiting for something to happen while your feet freeze, being a TV journalist can be exciting. At least I'm not assigned to Syria, Afghanistan or Iraq where it's open season on journalists. I've heard that the thrill of being in a war zone is addictive besides being potentially fatal. I'm not that gutsy.

Gutsy or not, I have to admit there's an element of danger. Why else would I buy that darned shotgun?

Chapter Seventeen: Heather in Danger

At the WMUP studio my police scanner lurks on the desk, the volume turned down to a murmur, but I recognize Charlie's voice when he takes a call. There was a 911 call from Heather Rasmussen. Joe Pascoe had been trying to kick in her door, the one with the strong lock Charlie had installed.

He did manage to get in, but Charlie and a State trooper had both arrived before Pascoe could do any damage. Pascoe recognized Charlie, of course, and cursed him out from the back seat of the patrol car while he was being driven to the county jail.

Pascoe could be charged with home invasion, breaking and entering, menacing, and assault besides breaking the terms of the restraining order. Concurrent sentences could put him away for a long time. That wasn't likely.

I didn't get home until after the ten o'clock news broadcast so it was too late to see Charlie that night, but we met at lunch the next day. I call it lunch, but it was just coffee, burgers and a salad at Wendy's at the edge of town.

Charlie was worried. "Pascoe's in our jail until he sees the judge, but the weird thing is, Kerstin, he blames you for his troubles."

I shook my head and dipped a French fry in the puddle of ketchup I'd squeezed out of a couple of those little unopenable packets. "Nobody accepts their own responsibility. Always blame somebody else."

"He says he's got pals and he's going to get even."

I shook my head. "For what? Is the guy nuts?"

But Charlie is familiar with the ways of the offenders he dealt with at the prison. He didn't tell me you could order a hit from inside, not then. He wouldn't want to scare me unnecessarily. "Just be careful."

What was I supposed to do? Walk around with that .410 slung over my shoulder like some UP revolutionary? No way. I sipped from my cup of ice water. "Pascoe's just a small town bum. Heather's little more than, you'll excuse the expression, white trash."

"Don't act high and mighty," Charlie cautioned. "You're a Yooper yourself. Folks in the Lower Peninsula think we're all a bunch of yahoo yokels."

That was probably because of a goofy band and a tourist stop where they cash in on the manufactured Yooper image. That stereotype was of yahoos who have no indoor plumbing, hunt deer on the sly all year long, and end every sentence with "hey" or "you betcha."

I apologized. I could see Charlie was sensitive about his own UP origins. I changed the subject. "So what about Heather now? Did Pascoe break the door?"

"She can get it fixed." Charlie listed the potential charges and ended with, "I think the judge will give him ninety days to cool off. I hope he has enough sense to go find some other girl friend."

"If anyone would have him." Ninety days? What about those charges? Was the judge a relative? So much for justice.

That was that, I thought. I hoped. I went back to the TV station. There were more important stories than Pascoe's assaulting his now ex-girl friend. That was the kind of thing for one inch on a back page of the local paper alongside the cribbage scores at the senior citizen center..

The whole business was getting on my nerves. Driving back to my place late at night I thought I might have been followed. I couldn't see who it was, just headlights, and I took another route than my usual. It looked like maybe I was mistaken. Once you start seeing shadows, they are everywhere.

The .410 was hidden in the broom closet and I was beginning to regret it wasn't more portable, like a nice little . 32 hand gun that fit in my shoulder bag.

Charlie had installed a dead bolt to my door in addition to the regular, rather simple lock, and I made sure it was secure and the blinds all drawn when I went to bed. Just to ease my anxiety, I parked the loaded shotgun within easy reach under the bed. That didn't settle my nerves at all, just made it worse. I had images of someone kicking in my door, too.

Nothing happened. No heavy breathing phone calls any more. Those had stopped after I put a block on the phone. If you didn't know the secret number, you couldn't get through to me.

I had a bowl of cereal and a cup of freshly brewed coffee for breakfast while watching CNN. I put the shotgun safely away. Before opening the door to leave I checked through the peephole to make sure no one was lurking outside.

Before I even got to my car I saw the tires were flat. They'd been slashed. Thanks a lot. There was enough fresh snow to hide the footprints of whoever did it.

Pascoe couldn't have done it. He was in jail. Maybe it was just some kids wanting some excitement by vandalizing people's cars. I went back inside and called the insurance company, a wrecker to tow the Taurus to a tire shop, and a cab to get me to the studio. I have comprehensive coverage, but the deductible of $250 means I'd have to pay for a new set of tires mostly out of pocket. I checked with Charlie. The tire slashing hadn't been part of a wave of vandalism. Mine was the only one.

I had to take a cab to work and told Queen Annie about the tire business when I got to the station. She suggested I should call that FBI guy and bring him up to date. The vandalism might somehow be connected with the subpoena. It was worth a try.

I still had G. Marshall's business card tucked into the corner of my desk blotter and called him on his cell phone.

"What's up Kerstin?" he asked in a hoarse whisper like he was on some stakeout.

We had hardly met except for coffee and a peanut butter cookie and he was already calling me Kerstin. Was he being friendly or did he have off duty plans? He's good looking enough. I wondered if I have a thing for men who go around with loaded guns. "My car was vandalized, all the tires slashed. I think I'm being stalked."

"Uh huh."

Tire slashing was clearly not in the purview of the FBI. "I don't know if it's because of Heather Rasmussen's boy friend." In spite of the hate mail, I didn't think it was related to the StopRape site. The postmarks on that stuff weren't local. "Oh, and I got a subpoena to be a material witness."

That interested him. "For what?"

"Seems like the guys who don't like their pictures on the StopRape site are suing for defamation."

"That figures."

What did he mean by that? I realized that Imogene Michener might have anticipated a backlash. Did she? If women victims could organize, why not the irate men whose pictures were posted?

And there I was, in the crossfire. Having a boy friend who is a deputy is a plus, but I still felt in need of support. I was hoping to get the FBI in my corner. I had to get him interested.

He was. "Have you heard anything from the Women Warriors?"

"The what?"

The tone of Marshall's voice suggested he thought I was an idiot. "Women Warriors United Against Abuse. Didn't you get a call from them?"

I was more suspicious than ever that he'd tapped my phone. Then I remembered. "Oh, yeh, hey. They were supposed to send me a brochure or something. Never got it, so I figured it was just a scam."

"You didn't check them out?"

"I've been too busy interviewing dog owners who abuse their puppies or covering the latest game for Queen Annie. Got to keep the local advertisers happy."

"Check out the Women Warriors and see what you find out," G. Marshall said. "Then get back to me." End of conversation.

It was clear he didn't want to hear stories about vandalism. It was also clear that he wanted me to do his work for him. Maybe he thought that since I am a woman I'd have a better chance to get information about the Women

Warriors United Against Abuse." If there was a membership fee, was he going to pay it? And if he did, did that make me a paid FBI informant, with all the risks that went with it, like being found in the trunk of an abandoned car in the long term lot at the airport?

My curiosity was piqued. I Googled the Women Warriors. Boy, was I surprised. The Women Warriors turned out to be a female version of a biker gang like Hell's Angels, except, according to other hits I found on Google, this bunch didn't seem to have a reputation for dealing drugs or similar criminal activity.

I'd heard about Dykes on Bikes, but there was no telling the sexual preference of the Women Warriors. Having excessive testosterone doesn't make a woman gay. It just makes her macho.

The Women Warriors all drove Harleys, so they had to have money. A Harley costs thirty thousand or more, and most of those seem to be owned by men in their fifties who finally got enough cash to live their Marlon Brando Wild One teenage dreams.

I certainly couldn't join the Women Warriors. I don't own a motorcycle and never even rode on the back of one. Nor am I in the income range to afford one if I wanted to. I was having trouble enough keeping the old Taurus in tires.

But I saw the connection Marshall was getting at. Women Warriors United Against Abuse were a perfect complement to the StopRape web site. Were they connected?

I shuddered to think what it must be like for an alleged rapist with his photo and address posted on the web site when he hears the roar of those Women Warriors in his neighborhood and sees them doing wheelies on his lawn with those heavy bikes.

Did G. Marshall expect me to join them? Me, Kerstin Mikkola, girl TV reporter, in leathers and helmet roaring around on the back of a Harley hog? You've got to be kidding.

Queen Annie might, but not me.

Sheesh. All I did was foolishly hand over a DVD with my two minute TV interview to an anonymous woman who called herself "Maggie" and my life has changed. We just can't anticipate the consequences of our acts, however innocent.

Chapter eighteen: The Women Warriors

To my surprise, the brochure for the Women Warriors Against Abuse did show up in the mail, along with another envelope with a one word message "bitch." Postmark Minneapolis. My name had reached that far. This kind of fame I didn't need, like maybe I was on somebody's list of the ten most hated.

The impression I got of the Women Warriors was of a sort of sister organization like the Shriners, do gooders who rode around on Harley's in parades instead of teeny go carts. Like the StopRape site, they gave legal advice but also provided tips on spotting victims of abuse. They said you had to be proactive and step in if you spotted a victim. Sounded good to me. Female good Samaritans on big motorcycles.

Sounded OK. There are other such organizations, like bikers for Jesus, for disabled veterans, or bikers who bring toys to the children's hospital, so why not Women Warriors Against Abuse?

The trouble is, there are all kinds of abuse. Eino joked that his wife nagging him was a form of abuse. In a way, he was right. I remembered that old movie, "Gas Light," with Charlie Boyer as the husband who is trying to drive his wife insane. I saw it late one night on the movie classics channel when I couldn't sleep. In that the husband doesn't have to raise a finger. No violence. It's psychological.

Then there's elder abuse, too, like Granny tied to her bed so she doesn't wander off in the night and ends up soiling herself. Keeping her from falling out of bed is OK, but not leaving her lying in feces.

At what level does that become, like the lawyers say, actionable? Nagging isn't a crime.

I decided to see just what membership in the Women Warriors entailed.

Turned out I didn't have to join. They had a web site and a Facebook page where friends could exchange notes, make comments, etc. I read them all, found a lot of self-righteous chit-chat.

Then I stumbled on a lead, a gal whose tiny picture by her Facebook comment showed someone in a helmet with a dark face shield. She looked, if she was a she, like Iron Man in the movie. She made a reference to sergeant Sauvenier, the snipped marine who raped Imogene Michener a.k.a. Maggie. Her cryptic comment was "we got him." Her screen name was "Chopper." That could be sinister or a reference to a kind of bike. "Get him" could mean anything from intimidation to murder.

My only knowledge of motorcycles is they make a lot of noise and cost a bundle. They also demand a certain kind of risk taking machismo. At eighty miles an hour a person on a bike is a projectile. Charlie won't ride one. He told me there are only two kinds of motorcyclists: those who have fallen, and those who will fall. Fall off and you may be dead. I guess that's why they wear those leather outfits with studs so they can slide along the pavement without leaving their skin behind.

Not my choice of transportation. Just give me a nice sedate ride. My Taurus can go over seventy, but on UP two lane roads with snow, forty is the preferred speed.

I couldn't tell if "Chopper's" comment was an editorial "we," a reference to the person who posted the comment, or a reference to the Women Warriors. Interesting. Besides chopping, did she also slice and dice?

Were the Warriors following the StopRape postings and picking out suitable victims for revenge? It was possible.

I learned that the Warriors were a California group. Did they roar up and down the I-5 corridor looking for alleged rapists and abusers?

I then surfed back to Google. Another search for rape stories turned up a sad story. A man who had been accused of rape and been mutilated, a euphemism for castrated. No doubt the news source didn't use the word castrated for a family audience. He'd gone berserk, committed an act of domestic violence. The man had threatened to kill his wife, held his kids hostage, and ended up dead. I could well imagine that a victim of mutilation might be depressed, angry, and even violent. But to end in a confrontation with the police? It's often fatal.

Charlie calls it suicide by cop.

It's an unsavory phenomenon and dangerous. Not willing to blow his brains out himself, someone provokes nervous police by threatening to shoot them. Sometimes they actually do shoot, and occasionally an officer is killed before the assailant is shot dead.

It isn't an unusual story in a country where men, usually white men of a certain age, just can't take it any more and go off their rockers. The story I found identified him as Carlos Wayne Sauvenier. That hit home. Like they say, the penny dropped. The newspaper report from San Diego said Sauvenier had an M-16 and aimed it at a policeman who came to investigate a report of domestic violence.

You just don't aim anything that even resembles a real gun at a policeman. Being a cop is dangerous, particularly in cases of domestic violence. Intervene and you become the victim. Many policemen are killed in the performance of their duties. They are so on edge that they just shoot. If they find out afterward that you had only a water pistol, well, too bad, kid. You're dead, hey.

So Sauvenier was dead. His downfall began with the assault on Imogene Michener. She was not your usual docile, intimidated, fearful victim. Posting his picture and address on the StopRape site was in effect an invitation for somebody to go get him. It worked.

It may have been a team of Women Warrior bikers who left him bleeding on his front steps. The trauma he suffered broke him. So now, besides a dead marine there was a widow with two kids. I hoped Imogene Michener was satisfied.

If that's what she wanted, the woman wasn't just a victim herself. She was vengeful and evil.

What was she supposed to do? Forgive him? "So sorry you couldn't control your violent sexual urges?" I don't think I could do it. Some Christians can forgive anything, but I'm not that Christian.

The government isn't very forgiving, either. Some see capital punishment as an act of institutionalized revenge. Rape used to be a capital crime in certain southern states if you were black and you smiled at a white woman, but not any more. In the cases when they are actually prosecuted and a conviction returned, rape might get you a jail sentence, but you didn't get hanged for it, not in this country.

In Saudi Arabia the woman who was raped was then stoned to death for adultery.

Joe Pascoe wasn't going to be hanged or stoned to death. In fact, I was sure Heather's report to the police wouldn't be followed up because she was his girl friend. They'd had sex before. Ultimately the only thing Joe was in jail for was violating the no contact order.

It was a good thing Pascoe was in Northern Michigan, and not in California. The guy was a jerk and I certainly didn't like him, but he didn't deserve a visit from the Women Warriors armed with nut snippers.

Then I wondered whether the Women Warriors were a national organization, not just a local California gang..

At least here in Yooperland with all our snow and ice on the roads you don't see many motorcycles. You betcha. But what if they had four wheel drive SUVs and a local chapter?

Chapter nineteen: Burgers and tears.

My car was ready. Eino gave me a lift to the tire store to pick it up. I hadn't bought a new set of snow tires before. The ones that were slashed were on the car when I bought it, used, so I was pretty shocked by the cost, even getting four tires for the price of three. At least, inside the heated tire store garage, it was warm enough to peel off that BITCH bumper sticker. Along with the shotgun, the tires were another major purchase on my Visa card. Ouch.

I like to pay off the credit card every month, for I have a dire fear of penalties and interest payments. I'm still working my way through my last student loan, which is why I don't own a new car or have a down payment on a house. Best I can do financially is that rented apartment in a remodeled old motel.

I called Charlie and over burgers at Wendy's I told him about my call to the FBI guy, and the Women Warriors. I also told him about Sauvenier.

Charlie had parked the patrol car outside Wendy's which attracted the attention of the other customers. Maybe they thought there was a robbery or something. It's not exactly a private place, so we took a booth in a corner and kept our voices down.

Charlie shook his head, "Sad story. Most of the guys we have to lock up just made a bad decision, got drunk, lost their temper. Most homicides are domestic. Somebody gets drunk and there's an argument. This Sauvenier let his emotions take over his head. Like you told me, maybe that recruit could do more pushups than he could. So he got mad and assaulted her. Stupid. One thing leads to another and now he's dead."

Souvenir's act of violence ruined Imogene's career in the Marines and now he was dead and his wife a widow with two kids. What a mess.

I didn't know Sauvenier personally, except for his picture and his posted dossier. I can't say I know Imogene Michener, but I couldn't help thinking that the TV interview gave her the publicity she wanted, and my face on the U-tube clip contributed. In a way, it was my fault for handing over the DVD. Guilt was trickling down on my head.

All of a sudden I started to cry. It was just getting to me. The threats, the hate mail, the vandalism and having to sleep with a shotgun under the bed were all too much.

Charlie reached across the table and stroked my face. With his buzz cut haircut he looks like a tough cop, but he's a gentle soul. He's seen a lot of meanness and evil and has to harden himself to handle it, but then he steps in to put a lock on a victim's door.

"Charlie, I don't know what to do."

"You want to move into my place for awhile? I got a spare bedroom. It's a big old house."

I'd been there. The home Charlie inherited from his mother was what the real estate agents call a fixer upper. It had been insulated, but the porch sagged and he heated with a wood stove, as anyone could see from the big wood pile out back. The carpets were worn out and the plank floors were uneven. It was a bit too primitive for my taste.

I wiped my eyes. There was mascara on the napkin. I'd have to redo my makeup. If I moved into his place it would be more than just a matter of convenience and safety. Charlie would be wanting more frequent sex. Next thing he'd be proposing marriage. I wasn't ready for that level of domesticity. "Not yet, Charlie. I think I'll stick it out." I added, "For now," just so he wouldn't think I wasn't grateful.

"What'll you do in the meantime?"

I sighed. "The FBI, agent Marshall, wants me to keep an eye on the Women Warriors. They're not around here. Just lurking on their Facebook page would probably satisfy him."

Now Charlie went into cop mode. "You think it's a national organization, or just local?"

"I don't know. But the law suit thing tells me that the alleged rapists are forming their own organization."

"There's no such thing as organized rape, except maybe in wartime."

I guessed there had to be a difference between a gang rape and an association of identified, alleged rapists, but I didn't say anything. I thought about newspaper reports from Bosnia and Africa, and the United Nations Stop Rape Now web site. There was organized gang rape in wartime, but it was a rarity in this country. We weren't at war, at least not here.

"Men in uniform think they're anonymous," Charlie commented. "They think that they no longer have any sense of personal responsibility. When they become a mob, they'll do anything."

"Sauvenier wasn't anonymous," I said. "Nor are any of those guys with their pictures up at StopRape. That's the idea. They can't hide."

Charlie agreed.

"Maybe Imogene Michener has the right idea," I said, even though I hated the consequences.

"She's only one person," Charlie said. "Maybe now that she's had her revenge on Sauvenier, she'll lose interest and it'll die down."

That depended on what constituted revenge. Was humiliating him on her web page sufficient? What about his being emasculated? But surely not the domestic violence ending with his death. What I'd read indicated he was not alone. "There are other victims," I said. "Maybe she's started a national movement. There's the enforcers, the Women Warriors."

"Uh huh."

"Maybe the law suit will get Michener to shut down the web site, or the web server may be intimidated."

Charlie shook his head. "She'll only find another place to set it up."

"Then there'd be no stopping it."

We'd reached an impasse. Charlie looked at his cheap digital watch. "I have to get back to work." He stood up. "Think over the offer to stay at my place. OK?"

"I will."

As he left and I thought of all those elements getting together in some sort of climax, I realized that this was turning into a really big story. Queen Annie doesn't want to run rape stories at WMUP, but the network might. This could be my chance.

Chapter Twenty: Network news

Before I went any further I'd better check with Queen Annie. She isn't just my boss. She's my mentor. I waited until after she'd seen the morning mail and had her cigar and coffee before I knocked at her glass door. I told her about the Women Warriors and Sauvenier's death by cop. I suggested, "This is turning into a major story."

"Not for us," Annie said. "It's not local."

"What about the network? I think they should cover it."

Annie understood and winked at me. "And you want to break it, get on national television."

Her quick understanding and insight made me feel naked. "Why not?" I tried to motivate her. "Might give WMUP a plug."

"And give you your five minutes of fame." Queen Annie shook her head. "Just don't let your ambition get ahead of your abilities, Kerstin. You may come up short. You don't want to blow up in front of a camera."

I'd seen that happen often enough. One ad-libbed blooper, one dumb statement maligning gays, for instance, and a career could be over. "Right."

"Go ahead and call network," Annie, said. "Pitch the story. As long as there's no national catastrophe like a terrorist attack on the White House, you might get on."

So I had permission. Great.

I turned to go but Annie cautioned. "Make sure you have your ducks in order. You don't want to come across as some yokel. Those big city folks who have heard of the UP think we're all dumb."

"Right."

As an afterthought she added, "When you're ready to make your pitch, rehearse it with me."

She was right, of course. I sat at my desk and took some notes on a yellow pad. I wrote down the Minneapolis post office box. The post office would have to know who rented it. I phoned, but they wouldn't tell me. The purpose for some holders of post office boxes was to hide home addresses.

Then again, why did Imogene Michener, if that was her real name, show up at WMUP? We're a long way from Minneapolis, eight to ten hours of driving in good weather.

Maybe the hate mail I forwarded to the Minneapolis PO Box was picked up by a partner. StopRape was a big enough operation to have several people working.

Some people think we sound like Canadians, what with our habit of ending sentences with "hey." Her accent sounded Yooper. She had to be local.

Imogene Michener. Was she a public figure? Her rape story had not hit the California papers. Unless there was an arrest, there'd be no story. Since her assault was on base and was dismissed out of hand by her commanding officer, her name wouldn't be mentioned publicly. The military were jealous of their scandals. Still, if she showed up anywhere, Google would turn her up.

Agent Marshall had shown me a grainy picture of her. Where had he got it?

After a foray to a house fire with Eino, manufactured home, one dead, dog saved, I edited the tape and returned to the StopRape story. I googled Imogene Michener. Turned out, there were several, a woman in Tampa, Florida who was a real estate agent, a couple of other Micheners who were too old, one of whom was dead, and a football player from Rock, Michigan.

Rock, which is an odd name for a town, is hardly that. The Wickipedia said Rock was an unincorporated hamlet along M35, here in the UP. Mapquest showed not much more than a couple of streets where a county road intersected M35.

Rock was established by railway workers in the days when the railway was king. Back then, before the automobile, there were railroads everywhere. There were no school busses. Kids went to school on the train. But after 1914 and the mass production of the Ford automobile, railroads gradually disappeared, making tiny places like Rock virtual ghost towns.

Rock looked to be too small for more than a one room school. The kids, if there were any, must be bussed to a consolidated school. Google found one, Mid-Penn. It had, in spite of the small, rural population, a football team. It was so small, that they might even let girls play. My first impression of "Maggie" who I now knew was Imogene Michener, was that she had the build of a football player.

Even a hamlet can have a web site, and schools do, too. It took a few tries but I found the consolidated school and an archived picture of the football team from their yearbook. At the back… sure enough. There was a girl on the team. That's where Marshall must have got the grainy picture.

If Imogene was from Rock, there wouldn't be many jobs. It was typical for small town kids, unable to find a decent job, to join the military on the promise of getting money for college. It was a ticket out of small town poverty. Considering our government's forays into Middle Eastern wars, military service was also a ticket to war wounds, PTSD, and a lifetime of disability.

We have a phone book for the entire UP. Rock's listings were less than a page. There was no Imogene Michener, but there was a Michener, John Michener. In a small town like that, all the Micheners had to be related. So I phoned.

The voice that answered was a woman.

I asked, "Is this the home of John Michener?"

"I'm Mrs. Michener, his widow. Who's this?"

I understood that some women knew it wasn't safe for the phone company to list their full name. Some use only initials. Crank callers and scammers look for the names of women in the phone listings. "I'm Kerstin Mikkola. I interviewed Imogene Michener for WMUP television. I'd like to do a follow-up."

"My daughter's in Minneapolis, but she should be back tomorrow afternoon."

Minneapolis. That's where I forwarded the hate mail. Maybe G. Marshall would have somebody stake out the

Minneapolis post office to see who came for the mail, but that wasn't a job for me. The Twin Cities are too far away, and I'm no detective who hangs out in a doorway for hours hoping someone will show up. But Rock isn't that far from my place, about a hundred miles. I could do that and be back the same day, weather permitting.

"Maybe I could come see her when she gets back. I have some important information for her." I wasn't going to tell her mother that the FBI was watching. If Agent Marshall knew who called me, he or NSA or some other Big Brother was listening in.

I didn't know how much Mrs. Michener knew about her daughter's web site activity. She might be in the dark, or she might be handling some of the mail, the email requests for RAPIST bumper stickers, or even dealing with the bitcoin account. Just because she was in Rock didn't mean she was some ignorant know-nothing Finnbilly.

What with the Internet, you could do business from anywhere. Did StopRape.com have an office? A boiler room of clerks? Or were the calls routed through Bangalore, India? That's why I wanted to go to Rock and not just ask Imogene Michener to drive up to the TV station.

Since Rock is in the UP, if they have cable service, they are part of our broadcast coverage. Queen Annie would be satisfied that this is a local story after all. Maybe she'd give me permission to take the time to drive there. I needed more information before I went to the network.

Chapter twenty one: Rock

When I told Queen Annie that Imogene Michener was from Rock, she got interested. "You want to drive there? You'll have to go alone. I can't spare both you and Eino."

Sarah—that was our weather girl—could pick up my job for a day. She was looking forward do doing something more interesting than talking about the latest cold snap, and Eino could coach her if they went out on a call.

A side benefit of the trip to Rock was that I could have dinner with my folks. The six o'clock and ten o'clock news broadcasts tie me up, so I seldom have much time to visit.

Imogene Michener wouldn't get back until too late the next day for a meeting. Her mother called me at the station and said Saturday would be OK. I figured noon was about as early as I could get there.

I phoned my folks and made a tentative date for dinner. They don't live that far away from my place near the old airport. Mom would have adequate notice to plan a menu. It might have been better to eat at a restaurant, but going out would mean my mother would want to get her hair done and fuss about what to wear. It would be easier for her to cook something at home, no dress up.

You'd think she'd jump at the chance for a dinner out, but she's unaccountably shy about public places. I don't think she's agoraphobic and she's not afraid of meeting people, but something holds her back that I never understood. My folks aren't very gregarious.

Anyway, it was settled. On my way back from Rock I'd stop there.

Queen Annie, as usual, was all business about the trip. "Take the camera with you," she advised. "Make sure the battery is charged. Get some location shots. And take a cell phone in case you get stuck."

I could hardly wait. Usually Eino goes with me in the WMUP van. This time I'd be on my own. At least, thanks to the unidentified vandals, the Taurus had a new set of snow tires.

Thanks also to Google Maps, I knew Rock was on the M35, but I wanted more information so I tried Google World. Google sends those little cars with periscope cameras all over the place. Turns out, they've been to Rock, too. Someone driving one of those Google cars with a camera on the roof had gone through the whole hamlet. There it was, not much more than a wide place on the M35 that runs north and south through the middle of the peninsula. When I enlarged the map on my computer screen, I saw a crossroads where a county road met the state highway, and a couple of streets that looped around.

The Google Earth Volkswagen's eye tour of the place was done in summer. The landscape at this time of the year would look a whole lot different.

Rock isn't much of a town. No sidewalks, nothing that resembles a city. It's just a few businesses scattered around, a couple of gas stations, a grocery store, and buildings that look like they were built a long time ago by carpenters without any particular plan. The only new homes look like double wide manufactured homes dropped in place. Had Imogene Michener grown up there?

Seen from altitude with Google Earth, Rock wasn't surrounded by forests, either, like much of the UP. It looked like a lot of bare rock which, according to the Wickipedia, was the reason for its current name.

Packing for a winter trip in the UP takes some preparation. I've heard of people sliding into a ditch, their car buried by the snow plow, leaving them unable to get out maybe even for days. Besides the usual shovel and flares I keep a long tow rope in the trunk and jumper cables. I have an old blanket, bottled water, and a basic survival kit. It would be an expedition. I even carry a bag of kitty litter which is said to be good for traction in a wheel spinning situation.

Charlie gave me the name and number of the captain of the state police post in Gladstone in case I had any trouble. I packed a sack of jam and cheese sandwiches, a thermos of coffee, and the remainder of a box of peanut butter cookies. I had the address in Rock from Mrs. Michener and told my GPS to go find it. I left on Saturday as the sun was just coming up.

It hadn't snowed for a couple of days and when the sun did come out it could actually warm the pavement during the day, only to have it freeze again during the night, which can be treacherous.

People in the LP, the Lower Peninsula, have little concept of what the UP is like. Even though M35 is a main artery running north and south, in the UP an "artery" means it's a two lane state highway and paved. There are no freeways up here unless you count a strip of the Interstate from the Mackinac Bridge up to the Canadian border at Sault St. Marie. Parts of our county have no more than three humans per square mile, and lots of deer and bears, of course. At this time of year the bears are all asleep and the deer are yarded up wherever some kind soul puts out feed for them.

It didn't take me long to run out from under the signals for the local FM radio station. My eyes were getting tired of staring at snow banks and scrub forest, so tired that if my GPS hadn't reminded me I'd have driven right through. I spotted the water tower, a tall blue post supporting a spherical tank on top like a giant push pin.

The single track of the CN railway which was the reason Rock was established in the first place, was being used by snowmobilers.

I arrived early enough to take some location shots for the broadcast and found the post office, identified by the American flag hanging listlessly in the still air outside what looked like a private residence. At least this sidewalk had been shoveled. No Saturday hours were posted but I counted a dozen old fashioned, brass post office boxes and a sign warning that people had to remember their post office keys.

Mail would not be handed over the counter. That explained why there were no typical rural mail boxes at the sides of the streets.

My GPS announced that my destination was on the right, but sometimes GPS maps don't coincide with reality. I checked my Google map and looked for Quarry Lane, the street where the Micheners lived. There were a couple of old houses whose original clapboard siding was punctuated by white plugs where insulation had been blown in. They must date from the eighteen hundreds when Rock was first established.

At last I spotted the Michener house. It was a dreary box of a place, painted grey with a front stoop tacked on. The satellite TV receiver bolted to the eaves told me this was not cable country. A note taped to the doorbell said, "hold button down."

I set the TV camera down because this wasn't an ambush interview. The sight of a camera might put off whoever came to the door.

The woman who came to the door turned out to be Mrs. Michener, Imogene's mother, a few years younger than my Mom. She wore a heavy sweater and an apron that looked like it had come from a crafts show, fancy flower appliques.

Some women are lucky and don't need makeup. Mrs. Michener was about forty, still youthful, but with a face that reflected some sorrow. I wondered how long ago her husband had died. She glanced at the camera at my feet. "Miss Mikkola?"

I can't remember when anybody called me Miss. "Kerstin. Is Imogene back from Minneapolis? We had an appointment."

"She's in her office. Have you had lunch?"

"I brought some sandwiches for the drive down."

"At least you can have coffee. Come into the kitchen."

I parked the heavy TV camera beside a recliner chair in the living room.

Whoever built the Michener house had been stingy with windows. The living room was dark with an assortment of furniture that, except for the recliner, looked inherited or second hand. A hissing, iron Jotul Norwegian wood stove, installed on a brick pad, wasn't fired up enough to take the chill out of the place. That accounted for Mrs. Michener's heavy sweater. The only thing new was a wide screen television. I mean, what else was there to do in Rock besides watch television and maybe knit a sweater?

Beside the TV was a photo of a man in uniform. On one wall a folded memento American flag in a frame and a plaque with a medal. That must be John Michener.

The Michener's kitchen stove was an old Sears Kenmore that might have been my mother's before she persuaded Dad to replace it instead of replacing elements when they burned out. A Mr. Coffee stood on the counter beside it. "I made you some fresh," Mrs. Michener said, and though she was drinking from a mug, she got out a real cup and saucer for me. Made me feel like a guest.

She sat down at the oilcloth covered kitchen table and I realized she was stalling. "Just what do you want to ask Imogene about?"

I paused deliberately while I sipped the coffee. I sensed she was trying to control the interview even before it started. I tried to be casual. "It's just a follow-up to the TV interview we did at the studio."

Mrs. Michener went to a cupboard and brought down a plate of cinnamon rolls.

There was the usual banter, "Did you bake these yourself?" and so on, to bridge the awkwardness. She wanted to tell me something but then again, she didn't trust me, fearful that I might repeat it. Finally she gathered herself and said, "This is off the record, like they say. OK?"

I put down the roll I'd taken a bite of. "Whatever you say will be in confidence." My fingers were sticky. She gave me a paper napkin.

She began, "Imogene's got what they call PTSD. She hasn't been herself since that business in California. Being angry and doing her web site helps her channel her energies away from what could be self destructive. You know, there's a high incidence of suicide among veterans."

"I know. I'll take it easy." I could have told her I had a subpoena to be a material witness in the class action suit against StopRape.com. That would have put me in the enemy camp. I didn't want to be any kind of witness other than a journalist reporting the facts. "I could use a bathroom."

It was upstairs. She showed me the way.

The bathroom was 1950's style, tub and shower, plastic shower curtain with blue fish. The sink looked new and when I washed my hands the water was hot.

Finally, when I got back downstairs, Imogene Michener, the girl who had called herself "Maggie," slid open a couple of pocket doors that separated the living room from the dining room and came out to meet me. She was suspicious and wary. Her first question was, "How did you find out who I was?"

I could have joked that we journalists know everything, that we have our ways, but I didn't see any point to it. "I had a visit from an FBI agent, G. Marshall. He had your picture from the high school yearbook."

She was puzzled. That Marshall was from the FBI didn't seem to surprise her as much as the fact that he'd found her picture. "I didn't have a picture in the yearbook. I never even saw a copy. I enlisted right after graduation."

"There was a photo of the football team. You were in the back row."

She nodded. "That was the year before. They let me in that photo but I never got to play in a regular game. Got kicked out because other teams wouldn't play against a girl."

It looked like sexism had plagued Imogene Michener all along. "Too bad." Unlike Queen Annie, I'm not a big sports fan. "Think of the concussions you missed out on."

Mrs. Michener was hovering. "That's what I told her."

A phone rang in the other room and Imogene turned to answer it. "We can talk in my office."

Carrying the cup of coffee and leaving the TV camera behind, I followed her. The dining room had been converted to an office. Old filing cabinets stood where a buffet might have been and a couple of computer monitors stood side by side on the table amidst neat file folders stacked in trays marked "in" and "to be filed." I spotted a stack of RAPIST bumper stickers.

She carried on her phone conversation in one word answers like she didn't want me to overhear anything important. I sat down on a creaky dining room chair, sipped my coffee, and waited for her to finish. When she did, I said, "I wanted to do a follow-up on the Sauvenier business."

"So?"

"You must have heard that Sergeant Sauvenier was assaulted." I hesitated to use the word "castrated."

She nodded. "Served him right."

"And that he broke down, was violent against his wife, and threatened the police with an M16?"

"I hadn't heard that."

"The police shot him. He's dead."

"Oh."

"How do you feel about that?" I wished I had the camera pointed at her when she got that news. If Eino had been along he'd have got the shot, but asking the questions and filming at the same time is so intrusive it intimidates. You don't get a spontaneous answer.

I realized, from what Mrs. Michener had told me that I had to tread lightly. I didn't know how fragile Imogene Michener was and what might set her off.

"I had nothing to do with it."

"Did you know Sauvenier was married? Had two kids?"

"No."

"Do you think the posting on the StopRape web site had anything to do with this?"

She shook her head. "How could it?"

I saw her left eyelid was twitching, not a good sign, and decided to drop the Sauvenier business. "What can you tell me about the Women Warriors Against Abuse?"

She was evasive. She didn't deny knowing about the Women Warriors, but she knew. "They're not my people."

Her people? So this was not a one woman show. "You have any connection with them?"

Her defensive body language was on the verge of turning hostile. "Why should I?"

I tried to make it sound casual and innocent. "Seems pretty logical to me. StopRape partners with its enforcers, the Women Warriors."

Imogene Michener sat down at her side of the old dining room table. She leaned forward and rested her arms on keyboard of her computer. "There's no connection between my StopRape web site and the Women Warriors."

Her denial reminded me of Bill Clinton saying "I did not have sexual relations with that woman." She knew of the Women Warriors and she knew Sauvenier's jewels had been snipped. She'd posted his picture and dossier, including his home address, on the web site. It was an invitation to whoever wanted to act on the information.

"Would you mind saying that on camera?"

"You betcha. I'll just get my coat. We'll do it outside. I don't want my office in your picture."

It would have been more impressive if my televised report showed a bustling boiler room of StopRape cubicles personed by a team of busy operators. On the other hand, how many international operations were conducted out of garages or dining rooms like this one? You didn't need a big office to reach out to the entire world.

That was a disappointingly short interview. Because the house was chilly, I hadn't even taken off my jacket. As an interviewer I had messed up. It shouldn't have been a hostile situation. We could have all sat around the kitchen table and munched home made cinnamon rolls, not just her mother and me. It wasn't her mother I had come to interview. If we had all had a nice, congenial conversation it would have established a better atmosphere.

We retreated to the front stoop of the Michener house. I hoisted the heavy camera to my shoulders, got the focus, and we started over.

To appear casual, I asked, "That photograph of the man in uniform in the living room. Was that your father?"

"Yes. He was killed in Iraq, in Faluja."

That explained the folded flag in the frame. That would have been the flag that had been on his coffin at his burial..

"We're a military family," Imogene offered. "My grandfather was an airman in World War II."

"So you wanted to continue the tradition."

"Yes."

"Until the, er, incident with Sergeant Sauvenier."

"I'd rather not talk about that."

I got to the point of my interview. "I understand that there's an organization of women bent on revenge against rapists whose pictures are posted on your StopRape.com website."

"Alleged rapists," she insisted. "I have no responsibility for any allegations. Hey, it's a First Amendment issue."

"What can you tell me about the vigilante group, Women Warriors against Abuse?"

Imogene Michener repeated her answer to my repeated question. "Nothing. I have no relationship with the Women Warriors."

She hadn't denied knowledge of the group. I couldn't think of anything else to ask her that would survive a studio edit. What was I going to get out of this? Twenty seconds of broadcast time? Nuts. Queen Annie would not be satisfied.

It would have been different if we'd been in a network studio with several cameras, not me standing on her front step with an intimidating camera on my shoulder.

I said thanks and goodbye to the Micheners, but before I left I took a couple of shots of the house and some more of Rock. It's not an impressive place, just a cluster of buildings on a two lane Upper Michigan highway. Thanks to a parallel service street you don't even have to slow down when you pass through. It was amazing that what happened in the dining room of that old house in rural Rock, Michigan, could go around the world and stir up angry women thousands of miles away.

I was afraid I'd driven a long way for nothing. Only later, as I drove north, did I realize that by broadcasting Imogene Michener's real name and location I'd put her in danger. Then I rationalized that if I could find out her address and use Google Earth to find her house, so could anyone else.

She might not have any connection with the Women warriors, but she might need them for protection.

Chapter twenty-two: An eventful dinner

Heading back north, I turned my thoughts away from Imogene Michener and the Women Warriors. The weather had turned cloudy and the brief thaw was giving way to our more typical winter. The wet places on the highway were freezing and the bridges, already frozen, lived up to the warning signs, "Watch out for ice."

My GPS reminded me to keep on the current road, but I knew the way and turned it off.

Fortunately, the old Taurus is a heavy, solid, road car. After a long day of driving, I reached my parents' home. They live in Ishpeming, an old iron mining town where the houses define the social status of the original owners. The rich and powerful had big, Victorian houses, often with a tower and back stairs for the servants. A couple of the most elaborate of those have been converted to bed and breakfasts for tourists. My parents' old house where I grew up is more middle class built in the days before air conditioning when in summer people sat out on the porch to stay cool and chat with passing neighbors on their evening walks.

My father works for State Farm insurance as a claims adjuster. He's losing his hair and when relaxed his expression has a look of permanent bitter disappointment. Maybe he's seen too many cases of people trying to rip off the insurance company. My mother keeps up her appearances. Her hair always looks like she just came from the beauty parlor. She once worked as a grocery check out clerk, but she has varicose veins from standing too long and now has a sit down job in the office.

"I made your favorite pot roast," she said brightly when I took off my boots and left them in the hall.

I didn't want to tell her that I was thinking of going vegan after interviewing a health nut for a broadcast. No point in criticizing a meal you haven't even tasted yet.

I don't make pot roast myself. If I did I'd eat it for a week. I'm not one of those singles who lives on TV dinners, but what with the six o'clock and ten o'clock broadcasts I have little time for cooking anything elaborate.

"What were you doing in Rock??" she asked when we got to the pie. One of the perks of working in a grocery store is you can take home something that didn't go out the door by the sell by date. This one was apple.

"I drove down to interview a woman who runs the StopRape.com web site."

At the mention of rape my father excused himself and retreated to the living room and the news broadcast I'd be doing if I were at WMUP at that hour.

His abrupt escape struck me as odd. "Is that a subject inappropriate for the dinner table?"

Mother averted her eyes. She seldom smiles and I have lately been aware that theirs is not a happy marriage. When you're still living at home you miss some of those subtle relationships. I guess it's like you stop listening when people aren't saying anything terribly important, and you take them for granted. Now that I'm on my own, I can observe my parents almost as if they're strangers, or people I'm sizing up for an on camera interview.

"Your father doesn't like to talk about such things," she said as we cleared the table and carried the dishes into the kitchen.

She washed and I dried as I filled her in on Imogene Michener and the Women Warriors. I didn't mention the BITCH sticker someone had stuck on the bumper of my Taurus or the vandalism on the tires. There wasn't anything to be gained by making her worry.

As she drained the soapy water out of the double sink and watched the swirl as it went down the drain, she confessed, "I never told you that I was raped."

That shocked me. "When?"

"You were just a toddler then."

She didn't explain the gory details and I was too respectful to ask. What with all the grim reports I'd read on the StopRape.com web site, I didn't want more of it so close to home.

"You know, honey, sometimes husbands react very negatively if their women are raped. The man can see the woman as dirty, damaged goods." She bowed her head, seemed to be studying something down in the sink drain.

Did my mother feel dirty, or was it my father's perception? It made me wonder how Charlie would react if I were raped. That could really damage our relationship.

Mom finally looked up at me, seeing me not as a daughter, but as woman to woman. "We haven't had sex since. He won't touch me." She started to cry.

I put my arms around her. I didn't want to pursue the subject any further. I wasn't going to ask if the rapist had ever been caught or if she'd reported it. I knew that most assaults aren't reported and of those that are, few are prosecuted. Convictions and real jail time are usually imposed on only the most horrendous serial criminals.

I admit that there's a growing awareness and more women are willing to come forward. The abuse of boys by priests went hidden for many, many years. It's painful to realize how much injustice and evil are out there in the world. Out there? Right here. Right in my mother's kitchen.

I guess my parents need some marriage counseling, but I doubt if my father would go.

Her revelation did answer one question: why I had no brothers or sisters.

"Tell me about those Women Warriors," she said. "Do they have a web site?"

"Sure. Maybe you could post your testimonial, Mom, anonymously, of course. You might help other women."

That dinner had turned out to be much more than a casual family meal. It had changed my whole attitude toward my parents. We had grown apart since I moved out on my own. Now I felt closer to them than ever.

I drove back to the studio to drop off the TV camera, edit the tape, and get ready for the ten o'clock. Sarah was glad to see me back, for she had a date.

It was a long day, and I wasn't prepared for what I would find when I got home.

Chapter twenty-three: Trashed.

If you let it get to you, with all the talk about rape, being a lone woman living out in the country when there are known creeps around, is a bit nerve wracking.

I was bone tired when I pulled the Taurus up in front of my ex-motel apartment. I'm the only tenant. The other two apartments fashioned from the old motel rooms are empty, so it's a bit scary to be the only person living there out on the highway. The landlord plows the entrance to the parking lot, so the place doesn't look deserted. He hopes he'll find another tenant. He doesn't live there himself. He and his elderly wife live in town someplace.

At least it hadn't snowed and I didn't have to shovel to get to my door. The add-on vestibule just has a flimsy storm door, and the enclosed space gives an intruder cover to break in. When I took out my key to unlock the door I saw that it was slightly ajar. Someone had broken in.

Maybe whoever had was still in there. It's dangerous to confront a burglar in your house. I don't have a back door for whoever it is to escape. Instead of going in, I got back in the car, locked the doors, took out my cell phone and speed dialed Charlie.

Charlie was already in bed. After all, it was nearly midnight.

"Charlie, someone's broken into my place. I don't know if I dare go inside. They might still be in there."

"I'll be right over," Charlie said.

My hero. He pulled up in front of my place in his truck about as quick as it takes to put on a coat over his PJ's. He brought his Glock, of course, and told me to stand back from the door which he kicked open, gun in hand.

My place was trashed. My TV set was gone, and stuff was thrown all over the place. My underwear was spread on the bed. Maybe they'd sorted it for a souvenir. Seeing my tighty whities tossed like that made me feel even more violated.

The laptop computer was gone, too, which meant all my notes about the Women Warriors and StopRape.com on the hard drive were now in someone's hands. My computer requires a password to open, but an expert can get around that. I don't encrypt my files.

It wasn't a total loss. I keep duplicate files on a flash drive which I can use at the studio or at home. That was in my purse. I suppose I could encrypt the computer files, but I'm not that tech savvy.

Worst, someone had spray painted the wall above my bed BITCH.

I was just too much for one day. I sat down on the bed and started to cry. Through my tears I started to gather up my stuff to put it away.

"Don't touch anything," Charlie cautioned. "This is a crime scene. There might be fingerprints and DNA."

"Oh." I jumped up like I'd been bitten on the butt..

"Did they take your shotgun?"

I hadn't looked. I had stashed it in its case behind a mop in the broom closet in the kitchen. It was still there. At least that was something.

"Better take it with you."

If someone else came in a new shotgun might be too tempting. Charlie wouldn't steal it, but I don't know about the other deputies.

Charlie checked it, saw that the magazine was loaded and the safety was on. "You'd better stay at my place tonight."

I didn't object.

Charlie called in his report and we waited in his truck until the deputy on duty drove up in the familiar serve and protect patrol car. They put yellow crime scene tape across the front door.

"We'll take pictures in the morning," Charlie explained.

I asked, "Isn't that a lot of attention for a normal burglary?"

"You're a special person."

I didn't think so, but he reminded me, "This may be part of something bigger, what with the graffiti, the vandalism. It may be connected with the StopRape business or that creep who got the no contact order."

"You mean Joe Pascoe."

"Right." Charlie started the engine of his pickup. "Except you can write off Joe Pascoe. The dummy walked away from a work detail. He was chipping ice off the courthouse steps and sneaked off to a bar for a beer. I guess he was thirsty."

I had to laugh. "What was he wearing? One of those insulated orange coveralls with 'Prisoner' stenciled on the back?"

Charlie laughed, too. "You got it. And he had no money. The bartender gave him a beer and called the police. Now he'll have to stay inside until his sentence is up."

"What a dummy." I now saw Joe Pascoe as a simpleton. Angry, but dumb. I remembered him slipping on the step in frustration as he climbed into his mud truck. It struck me as sad. Some people just aren't capable of real life.

I decided to call his ex girl friend when I got back to the TV station.

I followed Charlie in my car to his place. I was afraid he'd invite me into his bed. I wasn't in the mood for romance. When you're having sex you don't want to be distracted by images of a burglary.

Charlie's a softy for feather quilts, no surprise since he heats the place with wood. He saw that I was too shaken for any hanky panky and showed me to the guest bedroom. It's where he keeps his gun safe.

Nobody sleeps in the spare bedroom, and the bed is an antique single. I suspected the mattress would be lumpy. I was tired enough to sleep on rocks.

Charlie found me a hand-made quilt his mother had sewn, a patriotic one that looked like it was made of pieces of old American flags, lots of stripes and stars.

Charlie loaned me the top of a pair of pajamas and tucked me in with a brotherly kiss. "Get some rest."

Standing in the doorway, he added, "You might want to give that FBI guy a heads up about your burglary."

"I'll call him in the morning."

"Want me to leave the light on?"

"I'll be OK."

"You know where the bathroom is."

He still hadn't left. He hung about in the doorway with something else on his mind. "You know, Kerstin, it might be the time for you to seriously get that carry permit."

What did he expect me to do, walk around with a shotgun slung over my shoulder? This is the UP of Michigan, not the Wild, Wild West.

Before I fell asleep I remembered I'd better call my father, too. He set me up with State Farm renter's insurance. He'd know how to file a claim for the TV, the computer, and the damage. The front door jamb was splintered. I'd better inform the landlord, too. Maybe it was time to replace the old motel door with something more substantial, like steel.

Chapter twenty-four: Morning after

That mattress in Charlie's guest room was so lumpy I suspected it was a ploy to get me into his bed instead. I woke up feeling about the way I did when I camped out and discovered a stone under the tent. At the time, I'd been too tired to take down the tent and move it.

I was going to have to wear the same clothes as on the trip to Rock, long johns under slacks, typical UP winter stuff. At least I didn't have to sleep in them, thanks to the borrowed pajama top. I don't carry a tooth brush in my purse, but Charlie had a new one still in the package. He'd been given it at the dentist after his last visit.

After he inherited his mother's house he replumbed the bathroom with a new pulsing shower head. I emerged feeling fresh in spite of wearing yesterday's clothes.

Charlie must think the way to a woman's heart is through her stomach. Some guys ply a woman with wine or chocolate. With him it's food. He served me a breakfast of scrambled eggs, bacon, and hash browns out of the freezer, even an orange juice antidote for the nitrites in the bacon. I didn't know about the evils of nitrites until I did a health nut interview for the human interest bit of the news. I guess that thing about journalists learning a little bit about everything is true.

My place is only a mile from the WMUP studio at the old airport. I wanted to change clothes, but couldn't get into my apartment. It was still a crime scene. When I saw the patrol car parked in front I pulled in behind it. Another deputy was there doing the investigation. My landlord had shown up too, cluck-clucking over the damaged door. He said he'd get the jamb fixed. After some haggling he reluctantly agreed to replace the entire door with something more secure.

I called my father at the State Farm office and told him about the break-in. He agreed to drive out there and have a look, but he also wanted the information about the TV and my stolen laptop, like serial numbers, date of purchase, price when I bought them. I reminded him that, following his advice long ago, I had put all that on file at the insurance office including photos of the apartment. If you have a fire the insurance company won't pay for the lost books in your library unless you have a list of the titles. Photos can provide that. Near as I could tell, no books were missing. I don't think the burglar or burglars are readers. I hadn't provided information about the shotgun, as much so he wouldn't worry, as I simply forgot. At least that wasn't stolen.

I reminded him that the renter's policy called for replacement, not a depreciated value. That was his advice when he sold me the policy. Considering rapid advances in technology, a two year old laptop is virtually worthless. Maybe I could trade up.

Queen Annie hadn't been at the station when I returned in time to do the ten o'clock broadcast, and she wanted a full debriefing about the trip to Rock. The floor manager, Eino and I worked on the edit of the tape. It had been a quiet news night, no major sports report, so I was able to get in the Rock location shots and a brief voice over commentary about the StopRape web site and the Women Warriors.

Annie had seen the broadcast, of course. Though not overly thrilled about my taking most of the day off for one minute of news, she seemed reasonably satisfied. Rocking back on her old office chair and sucking on that little cigar she smiled. "It's not enough to get you on the national news, Kerstin, if that's what you want."

I countered, "A girl has to have some ambition."

"Just don't stick your neck out too far."

I told her my place had been broken into, mentioned the BITCH graffiti.

Queen Annie shook her head. "I thought you were a nice girl, Kerstin."

"I am, hey. It's just that some people have the wrong idea." I didn't think, I hoped, that this had anything to do with my comments on the StopRape face page.

Imogene Michener might stay inconspicuously in Rock, but the Women Warriors, it turned out, were on the move. When I called Agent Marshall to tell him about my trip to Rock, he filled me in.

Marshall told me, "It's turning into a national women's rights organization."

What did I know? I'm just an Upper Peninsula Finnlander working at a small town TV affiliate. "Imogene Michener says she has no connection with 'those people' as she calls them. If you missed the ten o'clock broadcast I can send you the video as an attachment."

"I don't do attachments."

I guess even the FBI, or especially the FBI, is afraid of malicious viruses and the like.

We don't archive the news broadcasts to stream for people who miss the regular broadcast time. "Stop in if you want to, or I can burn you a DVD and mail it. So what's this about a national movement?" The brochure they sent me read like PR wannabe fluff, not something particularly believable.

"There have been other incidents. Sauvenier is only one."

"You mean there's a wave of castrations of alleged rapists?"

Marshall actually laughed. "You don't have to do that more than once if you get enough publicity. Just the threat has alleged rapists across the country scared."

"I guess they can't just be defrocked by the Pope."

"Right, but there are secret organizations of pedophiles who trade pictures of kiddy porn."

Were there organized associations of rapists? Didn't seem likely. It's not that kind of a crime. There are no rapists clubs, are there?

Maybe there were. Wheels within wheels, I thought. There are all kinds of circles of friends, co-religionists, co-conspirators, skinheads, terrorists, right to life fanatics, liberals, Republicans, all manner of weird special interest groups, some of them sinister. What with the Internet they don't have to be a local group of old guys who have a regular breakfast down at the diner. They can be anywhere and everywhere. So, too, the Women Warriors.

I asked, "So what do you plan to do about the Women Warriors?" Not that I expected the FBI to reveal their plans and modus operandi.

"For the time being we just watch."

"You and the NSA," I said flatly. We've become a nation of snoops. Too bad they didn't see who broke into my apartment. If I were really paranoid I'd suspect Marshall had planted a video bug in my place. Some weirdoes even do that in ladies bathrooms. He didn't strike me as that sick, but you never know. A suit and tie might conceal a monster. It was a good argument to set up my own motion-activated web cam, except I have nothing worth stealing. As the saying goes, the horse was already gone from the barn.

Marshall's comments about a nationwide movement sent me back to the Women Warriors web site. Just what the hell was going on with 'those people' as Imogene Michener insisted?

Chapter twenty-five: Another firearm.

After my conversation with agent Marshall, I wondered if Joe Pascoe's ex girl friend Heather Rasmussen had heard of his attempted escape from the county jail work crew. I didn't know where she worked. When I called her home all I got was her answering machine. Maybe she didn't answer the phone. Maybe she was too afraid. I pictured her cowering behind that dead-bolted door. I could certainly sympathize with her. At least she knew who was likely to come to get her. I had no idea who decided that I was the bitch of the world.

Queen Annie did not want to give the burglary of my place any air time. A break in isn't news, even in this peaceful part of the world. Armed robbery of Wendy's, yes, but not some kid stealing a TV set or laptop.

I was preparing for the six-o'clock broadcast when Charlie showed up at the studio. He always looks great in that uniform and wide-brimmed hat. He had a surprise. I thought it was a big box of candy, but it wasn't candy in the recycled chocolate box. "A present," Charlie said.

It was a hand gun.

It hadn't been in his collection at home. Almost afraid to touch it, I took a deep breath and picked it up. It was heavier than it looked, but small enough to put in your pocket. "What's this?"

"It's a Beretta. .22 caliber. Favorite weapon of the Mossad. You know, two pops to the back of the head."

I didn't know. I wondered if it had belonged to some assassin. "Where'd you get this?"

"I have a friend at the airport. TSA confiscated it from some Chinese kid on his way back to Peking. It's legal. The owner won't be coming back. If they're not claimed, after a certain length of time they're destroyed, but sometimes they're sold."

"So this is legitimate."

"You will be subject to a background check, of course. It's the new regulation. Time you got that carry permit, honey. Be like half of the civilians in the UP."

I sighed. '*So it's come to this*,' I thought. I wondered how many harmless-looking grannies in the IGA grocery were packing heat in their shopping bags. What a strange world we live in.

Remembering Charlie's instructions from our trip to the Sportsman's club, I carefully inspected the Beretta, a little semi-automatic. I made sure the magazine was empty and the safety on. I popped out the clip. There were no bullets in it, but Charlie had supplied a box of them.

I put the gun back into the candy box and hid it in my desk drawer. "Thank you, Charlie. I guess you'll walk me through the paperwork and the application."

"You betcha," he said. "When you're free we'll go down to the sheriff's office and register it. Got to be on the up and up." His grin was forced. "You don't want me to arrest you for some violation." He would, too.

How much my life had changed because of that dumb interview over the StopRape web page. Now I not only had a shotgun against home invasion, but an assassin's pocket firearm.

That was the morning, but the afternoon was even more eventful. That junior lawyer who had served my summons showed up again. He was wearing the same topcoat and low shoes, black wingtips.

"Remember me?"

I took a deep breath, not knowing what to expect this time. Another subpoena? I didn't think I'd actually be called as a witness. "Sure. Except I don't know which side you're on, the plaintiffs or the defense."

"I'm just the messenger." He handed me one of those long, tan envelopes.

I opened it and was shocked. A preliminary court date was set and I was required to be present. I quickly scanned the rest of the legal language wanting to know if the case was being tried in San Diego. That briefly revived my fantasy about staying in a nice hotel and sunbathing on a Pacific beach. I was sure there'd be no trial in Rock, which has one church and a post office in a private home. Marquette would be convenient. Unfortunately, it was to be Minneapolis.

That made sense, since the StopRape.com PO Box was in the Twin Cities. Imogene Michener must have partners there who did more than pick up the hate mail.

At this time of year Minneapolis is even colder than the UP. Couldn't this wait until spring? Maybe the lawyers could ask for a postponement. Lawyers like to draw things out for more billable hours, like in Dickens' *Bleak House*.

I asked, "How am I supposed to get there?" I was mentally picturing the road map, winter driving through miles and miles of nearly deserted forest.

The messenger boy lawyer smiled, like he'd already made calculations, per diem, and expenses. "You'll actually be paid."

I detected a twinge of envy on his part. "You mean like some expert witness?"

He nodded.

I didn't think flying was much better than driving to the twin Cities. Since the airline mergers there's no direct flight from my neck of the woods. You have to fly south to Chicago first, change at O'Hare, then fly west to Minnesota. That could actually take longer than a direct drive through the woods. "I have to get permission from my boss to be away. Our news reports are vital, you know. Without WMUP, who would know about the bear on the back porch?"

"That's your problem."

I suspected that the date on the paper I was given wasn't firm. With court cases there were always delays and postponements. Cases can go on for months, even years. It made me pity innocent guys who, without being convicted, languished for months in the jail because they couldn't make bail.

Thinking of guys in jail I remember Joe Pascoe. If he had just behaved himself he'd be home free. The judge would throw out the dubious rape charge. His walk away for a beer would probably get him extra jail time.

The lawyer messenger left me to study the official paper more carefully. I'd have to tell Queen Annie, of course, and see if she'd let me go. It would be good if she'd make the case a bona fide assignment so I'd be on payroll for as long as the case took.

Then I saw that it wasn't just Imogene Michener and StopRape.com that was being sued. It was also the Women Warriors against Abuse. Maybe this could be network news after all. My chance for fifteen minutes of fame, Kerstin Mikkola, the girl reporter who had an inside track on a big story.

Chapter twenty-six: Woman warrior

I carried the lawyer's delivery into Queen Annie's glass office to report. She has a great view of the old airfield. Of course, big planes no longer land here. It's just for recreational aircraft, private stuff, doctor's toys.

Like a silent movie seen through the double-paned glass window, Annie was watching a little single engine job equipped with skis come down for a landing. It touched down with a puff of snow and taxied up to the base of the old control tower. One person got out.

The late afternoon sun glinted off the side of the little plane. The fuselage was painted with a private logo, a lightning bolt and a fist like the Norse god Thor. I'd never seen a plane with skis before. Could this be a story for Annie? Probably not.

"Look at this," I said, waving the legal document to get Annie's attention. "That lawyer guy was here again. I have to be there as a witness. Court will be in Minneapolis."

"When?"

I could see she was already mentally juggling work schedules. Sarah was OK doing the weather. She wasn't good at lugging a camera and doing one person coverage of an event. Sarah tended to stammer if she didn't have a teleprompter in front of her. Annie would have to hire someone part time, someone with a background in broadcasting..

"I don't know for sure."

Always the business woman, Annie said, "You'll have to use your vacation time."

"I was hoping you'd make it an assignment."

Annie shook her head. "Court proceedings aren't usually televised. Even if this one is, you can't hold a camera and testify at the same time."

That was true enough. For sure she wouldn't send Eino along. His wife wouldn't approve of him making a trip with a female co-worker. I couldn't imagine sharing a hotel room with Eino. His wife would have nothing to fear from me, of course. Old Eino is not my type.

We were interrupted by the arrival of the person who had got off the little ski plane. She stood in the open doorway to Annie's office and announced, "I'm looking for Kerstin Mikkola."

What was it this time? Another subpoena? With some hesitation, I answered, "That's me."

She slipped off a leather glove, gave me a critical look, and offered her hand. "Butch Wallace." She explained, "It's a nickname, not a category."

I guessed it was her way of saying she wasn't a lesbian.

She spoke softly, like it was a secret between the two of us. "I'm from the Twin Cities chapter. Woman Warriors against Abuse. Can we talk?"

"You could have done that with this thing," Annie said, leaning across her desk and hefting her old fashioned telephone ash tray combo.

"Weather's good. Needed to get in more hours. Licensed only for VFR."

I didn't know what VFR stood for, but I guessed it meant she wasn't allowed to fly at night. I hadn't seen a ski plane land at our airport before. I asked, "What plane is that?"

"It's a Cessna 182," she explained.

I wouldn't know a Cessna from any other make.

"Does about a hundred and thirty, but without the skis." She unzipped the flight suit. "These things are marginal in that cockpit, but too warm in here."

The flight suit she wore made her look bulkier than she really was. What emerged like a butterfly from a cocoon was a slender woman in her forties. Over her slacks she was wearing a shirt embroidered with the same lightning and fist logo I'd seen on her plane. This was a woman who did things right, no nonsense and proud of it. She had a set to her jaw that looked like she probably ground her teeth at night.

There was something exaggerated about the way she stood, like she was on stage, playing a part. Was she a caricature out of some Russian play, or was she for real?

Sometimes we become the roles we play. She reminded me of those road warrior women bikers. Were those leather jackets and helmets costumes, or were they really as tough as they wanted to look?

I could use a pose myself as a would-be network anchor persona, but hadn't a clue of how to look like anything but Kerstin Mikkola, Yooper, hey, you betcha and all that. I'm not like Marylyn Monroe who acquired that sexy look by practicing in front of a mirror. Anyway, a sexy look might work for Sarah the weather girl, but not for me.

Butch Wallace let me lead the way to my desk. I borrowed Eino's chair so she could sit down. She slung the flight suit over the back of it. I saw she was wearing stylish boots.

She wasted no time getting to the point. "Saw that you're to be at the court."

I nodded, wondering where this was going. "You wasted no time in getting here. I was only just now served with this paper." I held it up.

"We had advance notice. You got a place to stay in Minneapolis?"

I shook my head. "Hey, I only just got this notice. So why did you come all this way?"

"Could be rough. People may try to intimidate you."

I was confused. "About what?"

"Intimidating a witness is a crime. We don't want that to happen."

"I don't feel intimidated." Just to demonstrate, I slid open the drawer and took the lid off the candy box, showing the Beretta. I had no intention of ever using it. It was showing off, a bluff.

Butch Wallace wasn't bluffing. She grinned. "I like that. Me, too." She pulled up the cuff of her slack and pointed to the top of her left boot. Damn if there wasn't a little gun in there.

I am more and more convinced that the world is full of crazy people. Trying to act like I knew something, I asked, "Beretta?"

"Similar." She forced a smile. "Tell me. You had any trouble? I mean lately?"

I took a deep breath and took inventory. "Had a BITCH sticker put on the bumper of my car. Had the tires slashed. Got burglarized. My apartment was trashed."

That reminded me that when I got off work I would have to clean up the mess. The yellow crime scene tape must be off by now. Maybe the landlord would have a new door installed today. I hoped.

"You need a bodyguard," Wallace announced, like maybe she was self-appointed.

"My boy friend is a deputy sheriff."

"Live in?"

I shook my head. My sleeping arrangements were none of her business. I wasn't ready to cohabitate with Charlie. He's a nice guy, but I like my privacy. Occasional sex is nice, but long term intimacy means finding his dirty socks on the floor or the toothpaste uncapped. If I find any socks left on the floor they'll be mine.

Wallace explained, "I saw where you live on Google World. Looks like a dump."

She had done her homework, just as I had when I checked out the Michener address in Rock. We have no privacy any more. "It's all I can afford."

"Other units vacant?"

"Yes." My landlord hadn't found anyone as desperate as I was and willing to live out of town in an ex-motel.

"You do need a bodyguard."

Good grief, I thought, what next? Were the Women Warriors going to swoop in on me? Who was intimidating who?

Chapter twenty-seven: Bodyguard?!

Butch Wallace, however, gave me an idea. "Just a second," I said, and returned to Queen Annie's office.

Annie had been watching us. "Now what?"

I gestured over my shoulder. "She's one of the Women Warriors. They're part of the law suit I'm supposed to testify at. She says I need a body guard."

"You? I though you had that sexy deputy."

I shook my head. "This is serious. I think it was the Woman Warriors who castrated that marine who raped the Michener kid. The FBI guy says they're a national organization, not just a bunch of wild California bikers. This is turning into a big story, Annie. I think we should interview her for the ten o'clock." I realized I was excited and talking too much, too fast. I stopped to catch my breath.

"Think she might agree?"

"Why not? She looks to me like she likes publicity."

"OK. If she's willing, get a shot of that plane with the lightning bolt on it. Do it before the sun goes down."

"Great."

Annie smiled like the cat that swallowed the goldfish. "Maybe that will scare the bejezzus out of that Pascoe guy who threatened you in the parking lot."

I wasn't so sure that Joe Pascoe needed any scaring. His angry bullying might just be a front to hide his own inferiority. I'd bet Butch Wallace could stare him down even without her little boot gun.

Wallace said she'd be glad for an interview. She couldn't fly back to Minnesota until the next day, weather permitting. She'd have to arrange to stay overnight someplace.

I couldn't her offer my couch. She was too high class for that. Besides, I hadn't had a chance to clean up after the burglary.

"I'll check out those vacant units by your place," she suggested. "May send a couple of the girls to look after you."

She wanted to call a taxi, but Finncab has to drive all the way out from town. "I could drive you but I have to get ready for the six o'clock." Then I gambled and gestured toward the parking lot. "Take my car, the blue Taurus. If you checked my place out on Google World you know where it is, about a mile east of here."

I tossed the keys and she caught them like a bulldog snapping at a fly. "I won't be long. I can take you out to dinner after your show. Can you get away?"

Annie allows me an hour for dinner between broadcasts. "Sometimes I grab a burger or a salad at Wendy's."

She made a face like I'd offered her road kill. "I can do better than that. My treat."

If she could afford to fly her own plane from the Twin Cities, I guessed she could buy me dinner. I conjured visions of a steak at the Mather Inn. "Just so I'm back here by eight o'clock to get ready."

"OK Can we do the interview live?"

"Have to. There won't be time to edit a tape. It's a quiet news day. No big game to fill time between the commercials." I thought about it. "Maybe five minutes? Even ten? Not more." Most of the air time is sold to the drug companies who need seconds to rattle off the side effects of their miracle products. Always made me wonder about 'occasional death.'

Wallace stepped into those insulated flight suit coveralls and zipped up. "Deal."

A little apprehensive, I watched her drive my car out of the parking lot. Then I put on my jacket, picked up one of the shoulder cameras and hurried out to get some shots of that little plane before sunset.

Once back in the studio I figured I'd better bring myself up to date on the StopRape.com web site. I logged on and saw that there were even more alleged rapists posted. A couple of the men had captions imposed across their photographs, "withdrawn by request." By whose request I didn't know.

The most disturbing one was marked "Suicide." Underneath the picture the explanation reported that even though he claimed to be innocent the man had been threatened, bullied, lost his job, was blacklisted, and finally shot himself.

Imogene Michener's intention with the web site was to put some pressure on rapists, make them feel the heat. Not everyone can take it. Imagine if you were innocent and your face was broadcast around the world as a rapist or pedophile. The stain doesn't go away. No wonder StopRape was being sued.

The best defense was a strong counterattack and, thanks to the subpoena, I was in the middle: witness Kerstin Mikkola, Yooper yokel. That's how some people would see me, besides being a target for bitch hate mail, that is.

Now the Women Warriors were coming to town. They weren't just in San Diego. This was war.

Full of apprehension, I wondered if Heather Rasmussen would answer her phone. I dialed her number again. I remembered her number was blocked unless you entered a code number and did that. Then I got the answering machine. "You have reached…". "Come on, Heather, it's me, Kerstin Mikkola. Please pick up. I know you're screening your calls."

She did. It was a tentative "Hello," like she was uncertain, afraid, or maybe drunk or on dope.

"Heather, have you been paying attention to what's on the StopRape web site?"

She hadn't.

"I think it's time you pulled Joe's picture off it. You know the prosecutor won't take the case to the judge. Your rape claim is a she said/he said situation. You have a history of being Pascoe's lover. Are you sure you want to brand Joe Pascoe a rapist?"

She was uncertain. "Well, I…"

"There's a big law suit for defamation."

Heather didn't understand defamation.

"It's like libel."

She didn't know libel, either. I explained, "You aren't supposed to tell lies about people. A bunch of the alleged rapists are suing for damages. It's to be in Minneapolis. I'm supposed to be a witness."

She was surprised. "What's that got to do with me? I didn't lie. Joe isn't going to sue me, is he?"

I shook my head. "He'd have to claim damages and as far as I know, you don't have any assets worth going after." For that matter, as far as I could see, Joe Pascoe had nothing to damage, except maybe his family jewels if you get my meaning.

She was starting to wake up. "So what's this got to do with me?"

"The marine who raped Imogene Michener was castrated by a bunch of women warrior bikers. You wouldn't want that to happen to Joe, would you?"

"Gee, they did that? That's sick."

"It gets worse. He took his wife and kids hostage and was killed by the police. This is serious shit, Heather. I think you have to take down his picture. Withdraw your accusation."

I could hear her start to cry. I think she was drunk, one of those sloppy drunks who bawl. When she settled down, she said, "OK. I'll take it down. But I won't cancel the no contact order."

"You don't have to. He's in jail. They probably extended his sentence because he walked off a work crew to get a beer. He's not going anyplace."

She hadn't heard about that. "Poor baby. He likes his beer."

Breathing a deep sigh of relief, I hung up. Frankly, the Women warriors had me scared. Talk about intimidation. And Butch Wallace wanted to move in next door to do what? Protect me? Or keep me on their side when it came to testify?

Chapter twenty-eight: Dinner with the Woman Warrior

I had to set aside all those thoughts while I put together the six o'clock. Most of it was just reading the teleprompter and looking ahead during a commercial break. Our half hour before we cut to the national news is ten minutes of commercials, sometimes more. Sarah does the weather and I do the wrap-up of the headlines.

When Butch Wallace came back from the ex-motel she had news. "You have a new steel door. Your parents have been cleaning your apartment. I met your Dad."

"Oh, great. I dreaded going back there tonight."

"You also have a new key," she said as she returned my car keys. From the looks of the double sided brass door key the new lock would have satisfied Charlie.

"Did you talk to my landlord?"

She nodded. "We made a deal. I'll stay there tonight. Fly back home tomorrow. Now I've got to get my clothes out of the plane." She indicated that tan flight suit. "Can't take you to dinner in this."

As she was leaving she turned to comment, "You have a shot gun in your trunk."

So she'd inspected the trunk of my car. Butch Wallace wasn't just a pilot. She was a snoop. That irritated me. No doubt she'd spotted my long johns tossed in the backseat. That embarrassed me. She must think I'm a terrible slob. "Queen Annie is nervous about guns at the office."

"You should put some candy in that box along with your Beretta."

What with all the other action going on, I'd almost forgotten Charlie's present. Until I had the license I wasn't going to carry a hand gun, not even in my purse.

I drove us to the Mather Inn, the nicest restaurant I could think of. It's on the top floor of an old, renovated hotel and has a view of Lake Superior, which happened to be frozen. Wallace had surprised me. She was wearing a pretty nice outfit, a smart blouse and a jacket that complemented her slacks. She even had a necklace with the lightning bolt and hammer pendant. Must be custom-made jewelry. The woman had money. By comparison, I felt pretty grungy. I still wore the clothes I'd had on for the Rock interview.

The dinner was a chance to get background information out of her in preparation for the ten o'clock. I would have liked to run through some questions prepared in advance. She preferred not to talk about the interview. Instead, our conversation concerned my bad hair. She had suggestions.

Her own hair looked great. She must have a snappy hair dresser who knew just the shape to bring out the features of her face. She's a good looking woman in spite of that set jaw.

"Cut your hair shorter," she advised. "It wouldn't hurt any to lighten the color."

"You mean I should be blonde?" So many of the women you see on TV are blonde, it's almost a cliché.

She said, "You'd look good as a blonde," in a way that made me think that maybe she was hitting on me after all. In spite of her denial that her nickname didn't indicate an alternative lifestyle, maybe she was AC/DC. Naïve as I was, I didn't think there was much of that in the U.P.

Between the salad and the steak her conversation changed gears. She looked me in the eye and asked, "Have you ever been raped?"

"No."

"Molested as a child?"

"Not that I remember."

"Sometimes those memories are suppressed."

I just shook my head. My memory was of a normal childhood, playing with the neighbor kids.

"Know anyone who has? It helps you to understand what the Women Warriors are about."

The steaks arrived, twice baked potato. I could hardly wait to dig in. Averting my eyes, I said, "I learned that my mother was raped."

Wallace nodded. "I met your mother. She has that look."

Why hadn't I ever noticed? "What look is that?"

"Damaged."

"Oh." I'd have to look more closely to see what she meant. When we're close to someone, maybe we stop paying attention.

"I was molested," Wallace admitted. "I was thirteen."

I waited for her to tell the rest.

"He was an uncle. Dead now. Most molestations of children are by relatives or boy friends. You know that?"

"I haven't made a study of it."

Butch Wallace shook her head and gave me a wry smile. "I get it. You're a journalist. To you this is just another story."

"Not any more," I admitted. Yes, it had just been another story between the next car crash on the highway and the bear in the garage, but bears don't put BITCH stickers on your car or slash your tires, even Upper Peninsula bears.

It made me very uncomfortable to admit that I had become part of the story. I was involved whether I liked it or not.

That took the joy out of a nice meal.

We didn't have time for the Mather Inn's famous double chocolate cake dessert but hurried back to WMUP. While I reviewed the other stories we were covering, Butch Wallace gave me advice on my make up.

I suspected it was a rehearsal for how I was to appear if and when I testified at the trial.

Then it was air time.

Chapter twenty-nine: TV time

At least this time we didn't have to hide my interviewee's face as we did with Imogene Michener. Butch Wallace wanted to be seen. I introduced her and asked, "Tell our listeners about the Women Warriors."

"Women Warriors against Abuse is a national organization. We want to put a stop to the war against women."

I hadn't heard about the war against women. She explained that politically it went back to the fifteenth century. Women who believed in contraception and abortion rights were called witches and sometimes burned or hanged. She said, "If this were the fifteenth century we'd be called witches."

That startled me, but I did see the political connection. Some male politicians are so dumb when it comes to women you'd think they'd never passed beyond the adolescent school yard.

"That's not today. I mean, nobody's calling the Women Warriors witches, are they?" Bitches, maybe, but not witches.

Wallace tried another angle. "Did you read *The Scarlet Letter* in school? Hawthorne? American author?"

I hadn't. All I'd heard of Hawthorne was he was one of those dead white male authors the feminists had purged from the curriculum.

"In *The Scarlet Letter* Hester Pryn has to wear the scarlet letter A for adultery. She's publicly shamed."

I was ashamed for not knowing enough about American literature to carry on this interview without appearing stupid. I soldiered on as best I could. "Do the Women Warriors want rapists to wear a scarlet letter R?" I thought it would be sort of a joke, but she took it seriously.

"In some countries a thief has his right hand chopped off. At one time a thief was branded on his forehead or had a thumb cut off."

"So what are the Women Warriors going to do? Tattoo rapists with a scarlet letter R?"

"In some cases it's more than that. It's castration."

Oops. This is not a word Queen Annie would want spoken on a broadcast, even on the ten o'clock when children were supposed to be in bed. "You mean like Sergeant Carlos Wayne Sauvenier, the marine who was accused of raping Imogene Michener, the woman I interviewed yesterday?"

My God, it was just yesterday. So much was happening; my mind was in a whirl.

"Yes. I heard that a group of her fellow marine recruits attacked him."

"Surely the Women Warriors aren't planning to do the same to other alleged rapists?"

At that point she was evasive. "We take it on a case by case basis."

This was beginning to sound like one of those interviews I'd seen of right to lifers who threatened abortion doctors. Should they be killed? And did they have a right to their own lives?

This was getting too heavy for me. I was glad to see the floor manager give me the one minute finger. I wrapped it up and was grateful for the pause for a Viagra commercial. I missed the irony.

Butch Wallace had achieved her purpose and smugly retreated to a chair well off camera.

Sarah, who is a sexy blonde chosen to add spice to the weather report, did her thing. We were about to have a mid-winter thaw. Spring might be coming at last. By the end of May the snow would be gone, except for shaded pockets in the woods, of course.

Before the end of the broadcast the phones were lighting up. Listeners were pissed. I was in trouble again, or still. You'd think that by interviewing Butch Wallace I agreed with her program, her methods, or whatever. I'm just the messenger. What sort of hate mail was I going to get this time?

Chapter thirty: NRA "member"

Butch Wallace left the station before I could. I guess she got a cab over to the old motel. I escaped the irate phone calls and drove back to my apartment out on the highway. I saw a light on in the unit next door, but I didn't want to visit. I was wrung out. Butch Wallace is a person best taken in small doses and I'd had enough for one day. I needed a good night's sleep in my own bed, not that mattress full of rocks in Charlie's spare room.

I did in fact have a new door, a steel one, and a new lock. The double sided key fit. I carried in my long johns from yesterday and the shotgun in its case and turned on the light.

My folks had done a great job. My Dad had even repainted the wall so there was no sign of the graffiti BITCH. It must have taken two coats. Of course, the old couch now faced a blank wall where the TV had been mounted. My books, which had been strewn all over the floor, were back in the bookcase, though, of course, not in the order I kept them. I'd have to call tomorrow and find out my Dad's assessment of the damages for the insurance claim. It helps if your dad is the adjuster. He would know how to get the most out of the insurance.

I'd have to call Charlie, too, and stop in at the sheriff's office to register the hand gun and see about the license to carry. I had no desire to walk around wearing a firearm, but if the occasion came up I wanted to be legal.

Since my broadcast times are in the evening I don't have to get up early. The exception was when the FBI agent came in the morning. I slept in and when I got up there was no sign of Butch Wallace. I'd have expected a note or something, but she had vanished with the sunrise. I wondered how fast that little plane flew and how many hours it would take to fly back to the Twin Cities.

I called Charlie and met him at the sheriff's office to do the paperwork. I didn't have the Beretta with me, but he had made a note of the serial number for the registration. I filled out the form for the carry license, swore that I had not committed a felony, was not under a no contact order, was not mentally ill, and so on. I had to pay the sixty dollar fee with my Visa card. What with the shotgun and other purchases I was going to have a big bill at the end of the month.

Then, as if it were another present, Charlie went out to my car to put a sticker on the bumper where the BITCH sign had been. You can read a person's politics by their rear bumpers. "Honk for Jesus," "vote for Romney" and the like say a lot. Mine now has a green "Say ya to da UP hey" sticker. The one Charlie added says "NRA Member." What did that tell people about me?

I protested, "But I'm not an NRA member. People will think I'm a gun nut."

"It's insurance," Charlie explained. He had another and showed me. "Want this one?" It was one of those that say "You can take my gun when you pry my cold dead finger off the trigger."

"I don't think so."

"I'll give you one for your door, 'Insured by Smith & Wesson. Survivors will be prosecuted.'" He chuckled.

That wasn't a bad idea. My father had put stickers up around the house that said all valuables were registered and could be traced by the police. It was to deter burglars.

That hadn't worked and I wondered if my TV and laptop would turn up on Craig's list or in a pawn shop.

"There are lots of those signs," Charlie explained. "'Trespassers will be shot, survivors will be shot again.' Stuff like that, hey."

I shook my head. I hadn't known Charlie was an NRA member. Maybe the sticker was just to discourage people from stealing his guns. Of course, he was also a member of the sportsmen's club, so it made sense. Hunting and guns are part of the Yooper culture.

I'm a Yooper, but I don't hunt and have no desire to kill anything, not even whoever stole my TV and laptop. I don't believe in revenge.

I told Charlie about the meeting with Butch Wallace and last night's broadcast interview.

That she wanted me to have a bodyguard surprised him. "Sounds like bluff to me, hey. She's trying to impress you."

"I think she's trying to intimidate me. I'm supposed to be a witness in that court business. I didn't tell you. I got another legal notice. I'm to appear, but the date isn't firm yet."

"Where?"

"Minneapolis. It sounds like they're going to pay my expenses, put me up in a hotel, per diem, the whole deal." I squeezed his arm. "Want to come along as my bodyguard?"

He winked. "Will you show me your body? I want to know what I'm guarding."

I laughed. "In your dreams." Come to think of it, it's funny. We've had sex, but I don't parade around in front of him in the nude. There's nothing more intimate than the sex act and here I am being modest about showing myself. Go figure.

I could see my whole life was changing. Before the StopRape business my life was pretty straight forward. I'd gone from a Television major in college to the casino job and then WMUP. I had hopes of working at a bigger station. Now here I was with a shotgun, a Beretta pistol, an NRA sticker on my car, and a license to carry. What the H, Kerstin Mikkola, where is all this leading?

Chapter thirty-one: Aftermath

Thanks to the Butch Wallace interview, the you know what hit the fan. When I got back to the WMUP studio Queen Annie was well, intense.

"Castration?" she demanded.

I protested, "Wasn't my choice of words."

She shook her head. "This isn't an R rated station, Kerstin. Good thing it wasn't on the six o'clock."

I agreed. Considering her upset, I didn't think it appropriate to mention the hand gun and the carry license. It was too late, of course. Eino, whose eyes miss nothing, had seen the Beretta.

I was willing to bet he'd gone in my desk drawer to inspect it when I wasn't looking. Good thing it's not loaded or he might have shot himself. Eino is a good old boy, but he's not the sharpest tack in the box.

Annie gave me a stern look. "I don't approve of guns at the office."

I explained that though I had brought the shotgun in its case to the station one day, that was a fluke. Now I left it in the broom closet in my one butt kitchen.

"I mean that little hand gun in your desk drawer."

"Oh, that?" My act of innocence didn't work. "Charlie gave it to me. He says I need a license to carry."

"Really? Why on God's white earth do you need a hand gun?"

"I don't. Charlie says I need it for protection. My tires were slashed and my apartment broken into. I'm a target."

She rolled back in her chair, her forehead wrinkled with disbelief. "A target of whom?"

"Beats me. Someone who thinks I'm a part of the StopRape web site and all that stuff about rapists."

"Hmm."

"The Women Warriors woman, Butch Wallace, would agree with Charlie."

Annie looked over her shoulder at the empty airfield. "The little ski plane is gone. That woman warrior as she calls herself left this morning. Is she coming back?"

I didn't know. I hoped not.

"And what's this about a bodyguard?"

She'd heard that, too. Queen Annie misses nothing. She's not a micromanager, but she pays attention.

"She claims that since I am to be called as some sort of witness in the court case that I should be protected. I guess there are some very angry people out there." The phone calls to the station were proof of that.

Annie thought a moment, apparently decided that since I had a real threat and I had a license to carry, at least a temporary permit, she'd let me keep the Beretta.

"You may get your five minutes of fame yet, Kerstin."

"I'm not looking for fame."

Annie didn't believe that for a second. "Oh yes, you are. And you may get it yet. I got a call from the network."

My heart jumped. I wasn't ready for that. I'd nearly blown it at last night's broadcast. "No kidding?"

"You're to call him back." She slid a Post-it Note across her desk at me.

Was this opportunity knocking at my door? Or just more trouble? The name was Sasha Krakow. Sounded like a Russian immigrant, or maybe an Israeli who made good in broadcasting. I'd heard that Jews dominated the entertainment and broadcasting industry, but not at the level where I worked. I'd call him ASAP.

Annie thoughtfully lit one of her little cigars with that old Zippo and took a drag, blew smoke. "Being noticed could do us some good with the advertisers. The Women Warriors have shown up on the network radar. I don't think they'll do anything until the actual trial, unless there are more incidents of…" Here she took a breath. "…of rapists being castrated."

I didn't want to be part of any of that.

She could see I was reluctant. "Don't worry, Kerstin. You know the public. No story sticks around for more than a few days. Nobody talks about the earthquake in Haiti or the typhoon in the Philippines any more, even though the damage done is going to take years to repair. People have short attention spans and shorter memories."

That remained to be seen. As soon as I left Annie's fish bowl office I called the number of Sasha Krakow.

I got a secretary, of course, but when I said I was Kerstin Mikkola at WMUP returning his call, I got through.

He got right to the point. "You interviewed Butch Wallace, the so-called Woman Warrior, on the ten-o'clock broadcast."

"Yes." I wondered if I was in trouble because of the C word, castration.

"What's your connection? I understand you also interviewed the StopRape web host…" Here he trailed off, uncertain of the name.

I supplied it. "Imogene Michener."

"You seem to be right in the middle of this story. Mrs. Maki says you're being called as a witness."

For a moment I didn't know who Mrs. Maki was. Then I remembered that's Queen Annie. We never use her last name. "That's right. I got a subpoena."

"So you will be at the trial?"

"I guess so."

"We need you to cover that story for the network. The judge won't allow cameras in the courtroom, and might bar the press, but if you're a witness, you'll have a right to be there."

I could smell my big chance. A network story! Not just another chimney fire or accident on the highway. This was big, and I was in the middle of it.

"Can you sketch? Do quick drawings of the people when they testify?"

"Sorry." My excitement started to fade. Unless stick figures counted, I was no courtroom artist.

Mr. Krakow was still on it. "What side are you witnessing for, Miss Mikkola?"

"I'm not sure. The defense, I guess." It had to be the defense. I felt like a complete dofus. I had no clue about who was actually suing Imogene Michener. Was it one of the alleged rapists, or a consortium?

I was feeling like one of those journalists who know nothing about everything. This was the nothing part. We just put on an official sounding tone and stick a microphone in someone's face and act like we know what we're talking about. Then we hope, I hope, I don't say something hopelessly stupid, like "What is a boa constructor?"

Mr. Krakow told me, "Let me know as soon as something develops."

I agreed, but what if nothing did?

Maybe I'd better take the initiative, even though Annie didn't want rape stories. There was the name of a law firm on the paper I was served. Even though I had no zeal for appearing in any court case, it was time to stop holding my breath and go after the story. Like they say, poop or get off the pooper,

Queen Annie didn't like rape stories, but this was business. If this case gave the station some publicity and boosted the listener ratings, she might collect more in advertising fees. At least it wasn't WMUP that was being sued. That would be different. Then my job would be at risk.

I looked up the number of the law firm. It wasn't Lye, Cheate, and Steele, like on the Car Talk NPR radio show, but three other names that didn't ring any bells.

The lawyer I finally talked two was named Saunders. I restrained an impulse to ask if he was related to the colonel and told him I wanted to know who I was supposed to be a witness for.

Mr. Saunders, went into a part of the first part, party of the second part sort of lawyerly jargon. I guess if you write legal briefs you pick up the language.

After about five minutes of his declaration I interrupted and asked if he'd explain it in plain language.

Mr. Saunders took a breath and shifted tone like he was talking to a third grader. "This is a complicated case. Though Miss Michener is a Michigan resident, her web site is registered in Minnesota. The plaintiffs, the people who are doing the suing, are lumping the StopRape web site with the Women Warriors, claiming they are affiliated, that Michener is using them as an enforcing arm for revenge against alleged rapists. We're saying there is no connection, so one tactic is to divide the case into two, one against Michener and her organization, the other against the Women Warriors as some sort of criminal gang."

I was trying to figure this out. If there were two cases instead of one, the lawyers would make more money. Whose side was Saunders on? Why his own, of course.

"I think we can get the case against Michener thrown out with a summary judgment, dismissed for lack of substance. It's a first amendment issue."

I asked, "First amendment?"

He explained, "The StopRape web site is like a billboard owner who rents space and is not responsible for the content of the signs posted there."

"I get it. I read that in the contract. When someone signs up they agree that they are solely responsible for the content."

"Right. Your television station is not responsible for the veracity of the ads for Cialis or Toyota automobiles. If either causes harm, it's not your problem. I think we can get that part of the case thrown out on that basis."

It sounded like I wouldn't have to witness at all. I was beginning to be relieved.

Saunders wasn't finished. "The plaintiffs are going to claim that Michener encouraged, that is aided and abetted, the Women Warriors to go out and assault the alleged rapists. That could make Michener an accessory, but it's hard to prove."

It was all getting clearer, but Saunders wasn't through. "Then there's the case for defamation. Unless the alleged rapists are actually guilty, they can claim libel."

I countered with, "But Michener isn't libeling the alleged rapists. The accusers are. She isn't accusing anybody. She's just providing a platform."

"That's right. The plaintiffs are claiming a class action suit. If this were individual cases, each of the alleged rapists would have to sue separately. Not many would have the money or the fortitude to do that. Imagine, since you have only been accused, going on the stand to prove that you did not rape somebody. It's like asking for more trouble, since these are allegations. The plaintiffs haven't been arrested, in which case they'd have to defend themselves and risk imprisonment. Suing as individuals would invite arrest if the arguments went against them. Nobody will do it."

I was beginning to understand. "Then I suppose it's not a class action against Michener. It's an action against all those who posted their allegations on the web site, sort of a class action against a class action."

Saunders agreed. "I do not think all those people who posted allegations are going to get together and come up with the money to defend this case. They'll withdraw their allegations and drop out. Nobody wants to be sued."

I realized that if everyone like Heather Rasmussen simply withdrew their posting, Michener's program against rape would fall apart.

Saunders wasn't done. "The parties may go for mediation. It's a means of avoiding all the court costs and coming to some sort of mutual agreement."

Saunders' reluctance didn't sound like mediation would earn him many billable hours.

As for justice, this had nothing to do with justice. It was lawyers fighting lawyers while they collected money from both parties. It was like the stock broker who gets his commission whether or not your investment makes you any money.

The horror and nightmare of being raped was immaterial. The guilt of being accused or convicted didn't matter, either. It was all about money.

I felt like I'd been hit over the head. We were just like Christians at the coliseum performing for the audience while the lions killed and ate us.

I was beginning to hate Saunders. I didn't have much affection for Sasha Krakow, either. What Krakow wanted was a hot story. Hot stories built ratings and made money. It was network versus network, channel against channel. And of course, I was part of it, too. And here I'd thought that television reporting was an honorable career.

There was something called ethics. You didn't take advantage of people's tragedies, zooming on the mother's tears when her kid died, to boost ratings. Ethics, I realized, were in short supply.

So far, the only thing I got out of following the Michener StopRape business was trouble. I was feeling stressed and burnt out. At this point the best I could hope for was that the whole business would simply go away, that people would lose interest, that I would never be called, that I would keep reporting on bears in UP back yards and nobody would call me a BITCH for it.

I would hold my breath and hope it would go away.

In the meantime Charlie, my loyal, loveable protector, installed motion detector lights by my front door. If someone came around to slash the new snow tires, the lights would go on and scare them away. That was the plan.

Trouble was, the lights kept going on all night long. I'd jump out of bed, rush to the window, and see that a skunk or a coyote had come sniffing around the garbage can and triggered the light. The only animals that came around had four legs. No more vandals or burglars. Maybe the NRA member stickers worked as a deterrent.

Annie was right. To my relief, whatever furor the broadcast had stirred up was fading. The hate mail dropped off. I'd have nothing to worry about until the trial, if it ever happened, and that could be months away.

In the meantime I couldn't resist lurking at the StopRape web site and eavesdrop on the chats. The Women Warriors, too. Best that I'd not post anything, just hide in the shadows. No doubt FBI agent G. Marshall or someone like him was doing the same, besides the NSA, of course, which watched everything.

I told myself that, for the time being, I had nothing to worry about. At least, that's what I hoped.

Chapter thirty-two: Watch and Wait

As Annie predicted, StopRape.com and the Women Warriors fell off the public radar. Dad helped me file the insurance company claim and I upgraded to a bigger, flat screen, high definition TV and a faster laptop, latest operating system and a fat hard drive. I plugged in my thumb drive and copied the files to the new computer. My life was returning to blessed normal.

When Charlie came over for pizza and a cuddle he stayed the night. Of course, he set my loaded shotgun within easy reach as an excuse to stay. I didn't need it, but I let him play the role of bodyguard. I think it boosted his libido, not that he needed it.

It revived my suspicion that the reason some men wanted guns was they felt sexually inadequate. I wasn't going to test that theory! You betcha.

I wasn't quite free of the StopRape.com controversy. My subscription to the web site and being a "friend" on the Women Warriors Facebook page had consequences. It wasn't only the NSA and the FBI that were watching. The collectors of metadata were at work.

I started receiving emails from the second amendment crowd and catalogs for assault rifles and surplus military equipment. I could get a deal on a bulletproof vest and night vision goggles. I'd been pegged by my license to carry, which was public knowledge for anyone who wanted to look.

Right wing web sites and haters of Obama wrote me, too. It was amazing. Without intending to, I had tapped into a lunatic fringe.

What I found disturbing was the amount of hatred and vitriol that came through. Anti-Semites had fallen into the background, replaced by Islamophobes. Suddenly Obama was part of a conspiracy to hand over the country to al Quaida and replace the Constitution with Shariah law. This might have been a story to follow up on, but not for Queen

Annie. I don't think there are many Moslems in the UP and if there are, they probably keep a low profile.

What we do have, I found disconcerting, was the number of registered sexual predators. Someone had made a map pinpointing all the local sex criminals. Trouble was, there was no distinction between a genuine predator who survived prison, no small feat, according to Charlie, and closet pedophiles who'd been among the scummy international creeps who trade pictures of kiddy porn like boys used to trade baseball cards from bubble gum.

The sexual predators had attracted the attention of the Women Warriors, too. There was no shortage of targets for their vengeance.

Charlie says in prison a pedophiles' life expectancy is two years. I saw some sexual predators as sick guys who were unable to have a real relationship with an adult, mature person. Children were easier to dominate.

I discovered that a German kid who had used the TOR communication system went to jail. TOR shifts emails around the universe through a pool of member computers so they can't be tracked. Download the free software and sign up for the program and your computer becomes part of the shuffle.

I learned that the TOR program was devised by the police and military intelligence to protect informants and spies. It was quickly picked up by criminals and terrorists who wanted to evade detection. So the German kid's computer, without his knowledge, had some kiddy porn parked on the hard drive. Technically he was in possession and went to jail.

It was like arresting the postman for delivering a dirty book in plain wrapper. The tragic outcome was that, though you could do a year for stealing a car and were home free when your sentence was up, if you had to register as a sexual predator you were a marked person for twenty-five years.

So now the Women Warriors knew where the sexual predators lived. They didn't have to depend on the victims of rape to post the information on the StopRape web site. In the case of predators, it was public knowledge, there for the asking.

What were the Warriors going to do?

They'd be pretty busy. They had to be out-numbered big time. With that many potential targets, they wouldn't have the assets to post someone as my bodyguard even if I needed one. It was crazy.

There was a sad report of a pedophile who was registered and could not find a place to live that wasn't near a school, kindergarten, or church. He went underground, but when someone pointed him out, he had to move. His sentence hadn't been death, only a year in a county jail, put there because prison was too dangerous, but his reputation followed him. After several fruitless attempts of achieving anonymity he hanged himself.

Charlie is well informed. He's a good cop. He knows who is on probation, who is on parole, who skips those monthly meetings with the parole officer. He says you never know if the neighbor next door is a felon. They look like anybody else.

I suppose Butch Wallace would have had them all tattooed on the forehead or maybe sent to Devil's Island to prey on each other, not the innocent general public. How close were the Women Warriors to being pegged as criminals themselves?

From what I'd seen in my TV reports, there were so many crazies out there, the sane must be a minority. I'd told myself I was just an observer, a reporter. I wasn't involved. Didn't want to be. Now some people thought I was an activist. What did they expect?

I told myself to follow Queen Annie's advice. Let the whole thing blow over. People would forget. Trouble was, I still had the court case subpoena hanging over me. I would have to wait.

The remarkable thing was, the StopRape story had spread to other countries. *Der Spiegel* carried the story of a German equivalent to the web site. In countries where assaults on women were even more common than here, like Russia, a tide of outrage was rising. Women in India were rising up against the cavalier attitude of men toward rape and women's rights. Maybe Imogene Michener's tactic was not a failure after all.

Chapter thirty-three: The call of Spring

I tried to put it all behind me, to live a normal life in spite of sleeping with a loaded shotgun beside the bed. I went to the gun shop and bought a little holster for the Beretta, tried wearing it once, but felt stupid. Walking round like pistol packing mama is not my style. In my job I have to go into the courthouse, schools, and other buildings where guns are prohibited. The hand gun was a hindrance. It eventually settled to the bottom of my shoulder bag where it stayed like a useless lump, pretty much forgotten.

The Spring that Sarah had predicted in her weather report came on gradually. It takes a long time for our snow banks to melt, the temperature in the forties during the day, but freezing again at night. The layers of snow, alternating with traces of sand spread for traction, looked like horizontal rings on a tree, marking not the seasons but the blizzards. The last one came on schedule for St. Patrick's Day, March 17. It would be the last heavy snow.

The breakup finally came when the six inches of snow pack on the city streets softened and turned into ruts that had to be scooped up fast by front end loaders and put into dump trucks before they froze into ruts at night and made driving impossible. Frost heaves on the paved roads brought on a spring prohibition of trucks that would break up the asphalt. Unpaved roads were turning into mud.

Spring. Finally, all the snow was gone and the woods were dry but everything still looked dead. The UP bears came out of hibernation hungry. Bird feeders were as attractive o them as movie popcorn. We waited impatiently for that soaking, spring rain that would turn everything green overnight. That's how it is in the UP.

Spring also brought the phone call from the Mr. Saunders, Imogene Michener's lawyer. The case was finally on. I had to be in Minneapolis next week Monday.

Were the StopRape.com people going to pay the air fare? Would it be in advance, or did I have to buy my ticket and present the receipt, then play try and collect? I checked the airline schedules. I hadn't flown anywhere in a long time and was shocked at the prices.

I searched for the number and called Sasha Krakow at the network, hoping that in exchange for my covering the StopRape trial he'd pay the expenses. He had almost forgotten the story and had to be reminded. Was I going to be on payroll? Or was I to be freelance? He waffled. He would have to check, leaving me in suspense. Obviously Krakow was middle management, a job with some authority but much fear. It would be better to talk to the head of the network but that was impossible.

Queen Annie was not happy. How long would I be gone? A day? A week? She would have to find a substitute. Sarah had proved to be awkward when she wasn't in front of her weather map. She sometimes misread the teleprompter.

Annie did find someone to stand in, Larry Pelenpaa, a young version of a well known Finnish broadcaster. His father had groomed him for a job in television. With that family connection, he had an entrée.

Larry put on a confident face, actually came to the studio in a suit and tie. If the teleprompter got stuck, he could ad lib with ease. Did I feel threatened? I sure did.

Then I got a call from Butch Wallace. She was excited and full of confidence. She had passed her instrument flying test. She was no longer limited to VFR. She and some of her team would pick me up and fly me to the Twin Cities. No charge. I guess she wanted to put in more flying hours.

That was the difference between dealing with Sasha Krakow and Butch Wallace. Wallace was definitely an in charge sort of person. I speculated that she and Queen Annie would get along, but on second thought I realized that Annie, in spite of being the boss at WMUP, is a laid back Yooper like me. She's not impressed by people who are full of themselves.

A team? I wondered what Butch Wallace did besides practice her flying skills. Send teams of vigilante warriors around the country to scare the bejezzus out of alleged rapists, assault them? Kidnap them? Hell, that was a crime and not an alleged one. If I flew with them did that make me an accomplice?

When I told Queen Annie she loved it, but with qualifications. "It's like you're going to be embedded with the troops in Afghanistan." She sounded envious. "This is your big chance, Kerstin."

My big chance? Was she mocking me? It gave me stomach butterflies. I wasn't sure where I stood. "I've covered a lot of courtroom situations, but never as a witness myself."

Annie agreed, "That's right. You aren't just an observer. You're part of the case. There are pitfalls to being embedded. Your objectivity may be compromised by too close an association."

I nodded agreement. Being lectured by Queen Annie gave me dry mouth.

She wasn't finished. "I want you to do a good job for WMUP."

"You betcha." Of course I'd do my best.

"Just don't take sides. You tell me you keep an eye on the Women Warriors' Facebook page. What I guess they call being a friend. But remember, you are not one of them. You're working for me, not those angry women."

When I was away from the station, I would still be on the payroll. Still, Annie hadn't volunteered to pay my expenses. She must have been sure the lawyer for Imogene Michener would pick up the tab. After all, he was he one who named me as a witness.

What about the Warriors? What did they expect from me? I wondered if Wallace still carried that little gun in her boot. I realized that flying in a private plane meant she didn't have to pass through homeland security inspection. What did her "team", whatever that was, take on that plane? Assault rifles? Did they surround some alleged rapist's house for a big shootout?

Charlie and the other law enforcement personnel don't like rapists. If there was an armed confrontation between a rapist and the Women Warriors the police might just hang back and wait until the action was over. There was no point in being caught in a cross fire.

I dismissed the thought as a wild fantasy. All I was doing was getting a free ride in a private plane to Minneapolis. I had never flown in a private plane. That could be pretty cool.

My one and only plane trip was by coach to Florida to visit my folks in Orlando when they took a winter vacation. I had to change in Chicago, of course. I hated O'Hare airport.

I'd heard that of all the airports in the world, not one in the United States is in the top ten. O'Hare must be near the bottom. It was crowded and you had to walk miles and miles to get to your gate. When I did get my flight to Florida I sat in the middle of a jumbo jet, five seats wide and no knee room. It was not fun.

It wasn't fun, either when I did do a ride along in a helicopter with the drug enforcement people looking for pot plantations in the woods. That was scary. I was afraid I'd fall out or drop the camera and didn't know which was worse, falling out without a parachute or facing Queen Annie if I lost her camera.

Over the phone, Marshall said they'd pick me up next Sunday, so I packed. Standing beside the bed with my empty suitcase and my stuff spread out I was depressed. My wardrobe, such as it was, was strictly UP: jeans and lumberjack shirts and lots of sweaters. But Minneapolis? I didn't want to look like some yokel from the UP. What was I going to wear? And what about my hair?

I made a frantic call to my mother. Her hair always looks great. Could she set me up with her hairdresser? She could, and suggested that I lighten the color. Not exactly blonde, but something that brightened up my winter pallor and didn't make me look washed out. I admit at times I feel like something pale, crusty, and freezer burned from too much winter.

Then there was that wardrobe thing. TV broadcasts never showed me below the waist. For all the listeners knew, I might be wearing jeans on the set and be barefoot. I have some nice tops, couple of blouses, two or three sweaters.

Unlike Sarah, I don't wear anything that shows cleavage. She can do that to spice up the weather report. Sarah doesn't need a push up bra. I'm satisfied with what I've got and don't need to flaunt it.

My mother said I needed a power suit. She knows about office life, which is a lot different from the sometimes hectic and always informal goings on at WMUP. Mom puzzled over the color. Should my outfit be an assertive red, or something more subdued? What should a witness in a courtroom wear, anyway?

The UP is not exactly a style center for women's clothes. The hoity-toity style conscious wives drive to Green Bay for better clothing choices. Here it's Penney's or Wal-Mart, stuff made in sweat shops in Bangladesh or the Philippines. The only boutique caters to tweenies, you know, overpriced pre-stressed ragged cut off jeans with holes. I can't take a couple of days off to shop in Green Bay, Wisconsin.

Actually it was kind of fun to go shopping with my mom. It was a mother daughter thing. I wouldn't do it with Charlie. His idea of shopping is to look at shiny things in the hardware department, or guns.

Mom and I solved it by browsing in the local consignment shop. People with money clear out their wardrobes when the styles change, so the consignment store has top quality stuff that often looks like new. We got lucky and found a nice outfit that fits fine. It has a jacket and slacks, doesn't look mannish, but businesslike. If Butch Wallace really was butch, my outfit wouldn't look like an invitation.

The result was a significant but not radical change in my appearance. My hair is now off the shoulder, more of a honey blonde. In that power suit I look like I'm in a high wage bracket. That might be one way to persuade Queen Annie to give me a raise, that is, if she doesn't fire me for being away from the station. In this business there are always hungry new graduates from TV school begging for a job.

There already is one competitor, Larry Pelenpaa, whose grandfather was a major local TV personality who did the show Finland Calling, part of it actually in Finnish. There are still a number of Finnish speakers here in the UP and over in

Hancock there's a little college that used to be called Suomi, which is Finland in Finnish. They changed the name to Finland University, FU for short, which is kind of a joke.

For me, going to Minneapolis was a risk. If I screwed up, I might be out of a job entirely. Even if I got the story, that lawyer Saunders might leave me stuck with some major hotel and restaurant bills I can't afford. I basically live from paycheck to paycheck.

Mom wasn't too happy about my making the trip to Minneapolis in a private plane, but when I reminded her that the alternative was an ordeal at O'Hare she relented.

I called Charlie and asked him to keep an eye on my place while I was away.

Then I called Mr. Saunders, the lawyer for Imogene Michener. He was cautious, but I guess that's what lawyers are supposed to be. He reminded me that one of his planned tactics was to divide the case, separate StopRape.com from the Women Warriors. He wasn't representing Butch Wallace. The Warriors had their own lawyer.

"Don't let yourself be compromised," he cautioned. "Giving you a free ride to the Twin Cities may make them think you are beholden. You are not their witness."

"How could I be?" I asked. "I haven' witnessed anything."

"Yes you have. You said you are a friend on their Facebook page."

"Being a so-called friend doesn't make me liable, does it?"

"No, but if they want an endorsement from you saying they are just a bunch of concerned citizens, you might be useful to them."

That put another wrinkle in the business. I reminded myself not to be the naïve Yooper. Were the Women Warriors like the guy who takes you out to dinner and expects sex afterwards? Just giving me a ride in their plane didn't put me in their pocket, I hoped.

When it came to the trial, I had to be totally objective and not influenced. I didn't want to get too close to my self-appointed bodyguards.

When I asked Saunders about the hotel bill and whether an expert witness was paid, he was evasive. He said I wasn't an expert witness and not entitled to a fee. I'd been served a subpoena. If I didn't show up I'd be in contempt of court, might even go to jail myself. Thanks a lot. If I ever needed one I wouldn't want him to be my lawyer.

As for expenses, he said we'd talk about it when I got to the Twin Cities.

I told myself I was ready for Minneapolis, but ready for what? Was this going to be a performance like the climax scene in a movie courtroom drama where the key witness turns the tide? Or, more likely, was I going to sit there looking mysterious and dangerous to the plaintiffs' case, but never be called?

I've had my share of waiting around in a court room for something to happen. As a TV reporter I've had to hang out in the hallway with that heavy camera, waiting for the jury's verdict while the clock's ticking back at the studio. After all, didn't I drive for hours to Rock, just for what ended up, after the edits, as under a minute of broadcast time? Hurry up and wait.

What I feared was I'd get stuck in Minneapolis for days while Pelenpaa, my "temporary" substitute, ingratiated himself with Queen Annie. On his first day he presented her with a little box of cigars. If the assignment to cover the trial was a bust, it would be just my luck to find myself out of a job and stuck in Minneapolis. Hey, I don't even speak Minnesotan.

My other fear was that if the trial turned out to be huge, Sasha Krakow's boss would send some big gun from the network to brush me aside like I was the janitor or something. "Thank you very much miss whatever your name is, now step aside while the real people get to work."

Flying with Butch Wallace, a newbie pilot, didn't give me confidence, either. She'd just passed her instrument flying exams. When she came in that little ski plane she could only fly in clear daylight weather. What if there were clouds or it got dark, or rained? I was scared.

Chapter thirty-four: Meet the Warriors

I didn't realize that Butch Wallace and her crew had
arrived until I got home after the Saturday ten o'clock
broadcast and saw the lights on in the unit next door. She'd
followed up on the deal with my landlord. I don't see him
much now that he doesn't have to plow the parking lot.

You get pumped up for a broadcast. I had hardly sat
down on my couch to unwind when there was a knock at the
door. Butch Wallace.

Wallace is a no nonsense, get-right-to-the-point sort of
person. She had noticed the sticker on my door. Without so
much as a howdy-do she said, "I see you're an NRA member.
Good for you, girl."

"My boy friend Charlie put that on my door. There's one
on my car, too. It's to discourage burglars."

She approved.

"He wanted to put on one of those that say 'You can
take my gun when you pry my cold, dead finger off the
trigger.' I thought that was too much." I wondered if she had
an NRA sticker on the door to her plane. I'd try to remember
to look.

She was dressed in a matching two piece outfit in what
looked like cotton and comfortable, black and grey stripes. It
was a bit light weight for our cool evenings, but she wasn't
going out. She was just coming from next door.

She asked, "Are you ready for the big day?"

"It's not until Monday."

She cocked her head. "Sure, but we have to get you
settled first. Got you a room at the Marriott."

Oh, oh. I could hear Saunders cluck-clucking over that
one. I would have liked to say I was paying for my own room
and staying at the YWCA if they have one. I was still waiting
for that call back from Sasha Krakow at the network.

Saunders said only that we'd talk about expenses when I got to the Twin Cities. I was afraid it would be on my tab. If I were going to spend my own money on travel, I wanted it to be on a vacation of my choice, like to some sunny beach. This was a command performance.

I didn't know where the Marriott was and didn't ask for fear of looking dumb. I could always look it up on my new laptop.

Butch Wallace was being effusive. "How about a drink? Come on, I want you to meet the girls."

What I really wanted to do was crash on my couch, maybe catch the Tonight Show but I followed her next door. I was curious what she mean by 'the girls' and 'her crew.'

It was one of those early spring nights, a clear sky but moonless. There's a pond near my place, and I could hear the singing of the peeper frogs, all sexed up and looking for action. It was smelting time, too. After midnight the local streams would be crowded with people in rubber boots with dip nets and keeping warm on the bank by the heat of a burning old tire.

We are far from city light pollution. We have stars in our sky, brilliant, so bright you feel like you could reach out and touch them, even though you know they are millions of light years away. When I looked to the north I saw a greenish streak of northern lights. That's so awesome. It's like the earth is a space ship, the solar energies spread across the windshield like the fresh snow blowing off the hood of the car when you pick up speed in the morning. In Orlando that time when I was visiting my folks, at night you were lucky if you saw Venus.

I pointed out the Northern Lights to Butch Wallace and we stood there in the parking lot for a couple of minutes, mesmerized, before going in to meet her "crew" as she called them.

They turned out to be two women in their late thirties, Marsha something and Glennie something else. If I were a more attentive journalist I'd have memorized the names or taken notes. I figured I could I'd do that later, hey. There'd be plenty of time, you betcha.

The unit next door was the same as mine. I presumed there were a couple of queen sized beds, and the couch would make into a sleeper, standard motel furnishings.

Wallace's two companions must have been getting ready to turn in. Marsha, who had her black hair in a pony tail, was already in a set of striped, men's pajamas. Glennie was tucked into a pink bathrobe with big buttons and a belt. Glennie looked to me like one of the rainbow people, by which I mean multi racial. I couldn't tell if she was India Indian, Hispanic, or part Native American. Her complexion was dusky and she was blessed with perfect skin, not a wrinkle.

To my relief, I didn't see any guns. In my crazy fantasies I'd imagined a bunch of women like the girls in the Israeli army, all khaki and M-16 assault rifles.

Masha had a sort of southern accent, like maybe Kentucky, which suited her choice of liquor, which was sour mash bourbon. She had a bottle and glasses, but I turned that down. "Got any beer?" I'd do that much just to be sociable.

They did, Coors Light from the fridge. I skipped the proffered glass, drank from the can.

"So what happens tomorrow?" I asked, as I sat at the table for two by the front window. The curtains were closed.

"Weather's good. We'll take off after breakfast."

I had no problem with that. She said it would take about four hours to fly to the Twin Cities. The Cessna didn't have the range to do the trip in one hop. They'd have to land on the way to refuel and take a potty break.

Sasha and Glennie had other local plans besides just picking me up. Their idea of sight seeing on Sunday morning was to scope out the local pervs, as Sasha put it. They had a map marked with the locations of all the local registered sex offenders.

I thought about Sgt. Sauvenier and his mutilation. What were these women? Trophy hunters, like the Vietnam vets Charlie's dad told him about who collected Viet Kong ears as souvenirs? I shuddered to think about it.

Sasha and Glennie looked like a couple of housewives. Did they have kids at home and husbands? Was hunting down the "pervs" a kind of sport? Or did they see themselves as vindictive, angry vigilantes, cleaning up the neighborhoods of scum when the courts and jails failed?

The KKK had been motivated by hatred of people not white and Jews. I guessed there could be a lot of excuses for hatred, to blame others for one's own failures or inadequacies. It was hard for me to figure these women out.

I hadn't seen a rental car outside. What did they expect to do, cruise the town in a cab? More likely they'd enlist me as driver, a sort of hunting guide. No wonder they were being sued.

Glennie said, "You have a local rapist, too. Some jerk named Pascoe." She showed me their treasure map, X marks the spot out on one of the county roads. I hadn't known where he lived, when he wasn't in jail, of course.

"Joe Pascoe," I explained. "He's not a rapist. The prosecutor wouldn't follow up on that charge. He's in jail now for violating a no contact order. Tried to break into his girl friend's place out by the old air base. My boy friend arrested him."

"Your boy friend?"

"Charlie Johnson. He's a deputy sheriff."

Glennie said, "Must be nice."

Sasha commented, "It would be handy to have a pet cop."

That rankled. There was no reason to belittle Charlie Johnson. "He's not a pet. He's my boy friend." But I admitted it was useful for a TV reporter to know someone who was a cop. I told them we'd met while I was covering an accident on the highway.

I was afraid Butch would ask me if I had sex with Charlie. She gave me that look, but kept her mouth shut.

Glennie wanted to know more about Pascoe.

I was glad to change the subject from Charlie. I held up my can of Coors. "Couldn't resist beer. Walked away from a work crew at the court house to get a cool one and got arrested for trying to escape. They must have extended his sentence. He's still in the county jail, so far as I know."

"Too bad," Masha said. I couldn't tell if it was too bad that he was in jail or too bad that he wasn't out.

It reminded me that I'd told Heather Rasmussen she should take Pascoe off the StopRape list of allegeds. I'd have to call her. I hoped she wasn't still mad at him. She'd had several months to reconsider.

Wallace commented on my new hair color and I told her I had a power suit to wear in court. She also wanted to know if I would take along my Beretta.

I asked, "Why would I do that? I thought these are my bodyguards." I gestured to Masha and Glennie. They didn't look athletic or tough, but firearms are equalizers, as the cowboys said in the Wild West. Did they carry little guns in their boots? Or maybe their garter belts? I couldn't imagine them in leathers on hog Harleys roaring up and down the street outside some "perv's" house to intimidate him. You never know. Put on a rubber nose and big shoes and suddenly you're a clown.

Those women made me nervous. I was reminded of what Charlie said about the murderers in Marquette prison when he was a guard. They look like anybody else, even better, like that handsome George Bundy who killed all those girls.

With all those things going on in my head I wasn't exactly looking forward to the flight to Minneapolis. I'd be in a strange place, with somewhat sinister people, little cash, while my job was under advisement back home. Even if I did carry the little gun I wouldn't have much confidence.

Chapter thirty-five: Flight to Minnesota

We were to fly out on Sunday, but first the Warriors needed breakfast. There's no restaurant at the old airport terminal which had been converted to the WMUP studio. When commercial planes did land there were only about four flights a day, no justification for a restaurant. Back then the only food came out of vending machines, candy bars, chips, and sodas. Now even those machines were gone. That's why I had my so-called lunch at Wendy's on the edge of town.

I wasn't about to do breakfast for three unexpected visitors. They weren't my guests, after all. I didn't buy Butch Wallace's story that I needed a bodyguard, and certainly not three. They wanted me for something. They weren't like G. Marshall, that polite FBI agent, who left his shoes at the door, drank my coffee and was satisfied with a couple of stale, store-bought peanut butter cookies. Sunday would be brunch, and I felt obliged to be the driver.

We all piled into my Taurus and I took them into Marquette, the snow tires singing on the now clear and dry pavement. With their map guide to local registered sex offenders on Glennie's lap in the front seat, I got a tour of neighborhoods I'd frankly never seen.

The women knew about that BITCH sticker that had been put on my bumper. Glennie figured it was one of those offenders marked on her map, but I wasn't about to go knocking at doors and asking if someone had put a nasty bumper sticker on my car. I'm not that confrontational, not like those Women Warriors.

I suppose, by process of elimination, you could go through the list of those names on their map and compare it with those posted on the web site, but it hardly seemed worth the trouble just because of a sticker As for the tire slashing episode, how could I prove anything? And the burglary might not have any connection at all. My motel apartment was exposed on the highway and easy pickings.

Masha, in the back seat, took digital photos of the houses where the registered sex offenders lived. Were Women Warriors across the country doing the same thing? They also wanted to see where Pascoe lived. The frost warnings were still in effect, and you could see how the pavement had heaved and buckled on the local, paved road. Then we were into gravel that gave way at times to muddy ruts where springs welled up.

When they set up 911 services here in the UP every road with more than one house had to be named. The old fire numbers were no longer quite enough in case of an emergency. Fire numbers didn't get on county maps, but named roads did. It was one way to get the county to plow in the winter, no road name, no service. Considering the cost of maintaining our roads in winter, plowing was a bargain for the property tax.

I had never been there, but guessed that Pascoe's place was back on a nameless two track. It was. It looked solid enough, that looks can be deceiving.. We hadn't gone a hundred yards before I could feel the wheels slipping and sliding. "I'm not doing this," I said. "This isn't a four wheel drive, hey." The two track hadn't been driven on. The surface was like grease on top of chocolate pudding. If I kept going, we were bound to get stuck. Who would find us back there? Nobody. We'd have to use a cell phone to call a wrecker, if we were in range of a signal, that is.

On the edge of panic, I stopped very gently and gingerly backed out onto the gravel road. "He's in jail anyway," I said. "No point in going back there."

Hopeful, Masha suggested, "Google World probably has a view of the place."

I couldn't imagine the Google car with its periscope camera would venture back there. Even cruising Rock had to be stretching it a bit.

We returned to the main road. When I accelerated, the snow tires flung the accumulated mud off, rattling the wheel wells. I chauffeured the Warriors to the Mather Inn for their Sunday brunch. As we got out of my car in the parking lot I looked up and saw a grey overcast moving in from the west. I hadn't paid much attention to Sarah when she was doing her thing the night before, but I did remember one word: rain.

Butch Wallace noticed it, too, and she was noticeably nervous. "I think we'd better go," she said while we still hadn't finished our waffles and scrambled eggs.

I wanted to pay for my own breakfast, be independent. Butch had already paid. I was becoming more and more beholden to these people.

I drove us back to my place at the old motel to pick up our luggage.

I was nervous, leaving my apartment. I had hidden the shotgun in the broom closet again. Even though I could have taken it on the plane, I didn't think I'd need it, so I slipped the Beretta under the mattress. I took a last look before locking the new, steel door. When would I be back?

Then it was the last mile to the old airport and WMUP.

Queen Annie was in. I saw her watching as the three Women Warriors walked over to the Cessna with its lightning bolt and fist insignia. I stopped in for final instructions.

Annie was dressed for Sunday church. She'd hoped to see me off. "Too bad you can't take one of the station cameras," she said. "They're too bulky. But I have a little one, I think you've used these before." She handed me a video camera with the WMUP logo sticker on the side. It was the same kind I'd used in TV school. They have a gyroscopic feature to dampen the otherwise inevitable shaking.

I examined it. "No problem."

"Take a spare battery pack."

Queen Annie gave me a motherly look. I saw her as my mentor. She wasn't just my boss. I could see she was worried.

So was I.

I was worried about what was going to be at the trial, how I was to handle the expenses, who was going to pay, and, first of all, was Butch Wallace capable of flying in bad weather?

I'd never had to worry about weight aboard an airplane. The video camera and my laptop in its case, plus my carry-on were pretty bulky. Fortunately none of the three women were fat. I watched as Masha and Glennie stowed the luggage. Would we get off the ground with all that stuff?

The Cessna was hardly your executive jet. Butch put me in the co-pilot's seat in front so I would have a better view and use the video camera. I fastened my seat belt and held the video recorder on my lap.

Butch went through her pre-flight checklist. The single engine started smoothly and before I realized it we were taxing down the runway. We picked up speed, but with four people in that little plane we were pretty heavy. I could see the trees at the end of the runway coming closer and held my breath. I was pretty nervous and suddenly realized I should have made a pit stop before we took off. Could I hold it until we stopped to refuel? Then we were off the ground, circling west toward Wisconsin and on to Minnesota.

Fortunately flying today isn't like those first air mail pilots who followed roads or rivers and even big concrete arrows set into fields at intervals so they could find their way across country. Now there are radio beacons and GPS. Butch always knew where we were, even when we closed in on the overcast, with rain spraying the windshield, and tried to climb above the clouds. The Cessna wasn't pressurized, so we had to stay under ten thousand feet, which I could see on the little dial. Luckily we broke through the clouds before that and it was smooth going.

By the time the butterflies in my stomach settled down we had dropped down through the layer of clouds and were looking for the air strip to refuel. From my front seat the runway looked tiny when I did finally spot it through the rain. I held my breath as the Cessna swayed before that little hesitation. I guess the pilot's trick is to get real close and then sort of stall at the right moment and drop nice and easy onto the runway. We bounced once. Then we were down and I breathed again.

I don't know what airport it was, probably Iron River, but I sure found that bathroom, just in time.

Butch got a cup of coffee from a vending machine but I took a pass. Caffeine is a diuretic and I didn't want to have to pee again.

We were on the ground no more than half an hour before we took off again. This time I sat in back with Masha. Wanted to interview her, take some notes. I got her last name, her home town, which turned out to be a suburb of Minneapolis. Her reason for joining the Women Warriors? A friend had been raped and murdered. The killer hadn't been caught yet. For Masha, joining the Women Warriors was more proactive than sitting around mourning the loss of her best friend. She didn't own a Harley motorcycle. There were some road warriors on bikes in Minnesota, but she wasn't one of that bunch.

I knew from the Facebook site that the Warriors had formed a national organization and even had a couple of foreign affiliates. It wasn't just an ad hoc temporary hook up of people with a similar interest. They had chapters and officers.

That was quite different from Imogene Michener's web site with its paid subscribers. Imogene was assisted by volunteers, someone to pick up the mail in Minneapolis, a web master, and of course Mr. Saunders, her lawyer. No wonder his plan was to separate the legal situation into two separate lawsuits. He wanted no part of the Warriors who he saw as stalkers or worse.

I didn't know who the lawyer was representing the Women Warriors. No doubt I'd meet him or her soon.

We didn't land at the big commercial airport in Minneapolis, but a small one outside of town. The rain had stopped and, typical after a front passed, the wind was gusty and we bounced around. It felt like we were barely under control. Butch came in too fast on her first attempt to land, had to fly around and try again. By that time I was a nervous wreck. I was the last one out of the plane and unsteady on my feet. At least I wasn't sick. The Cessna didn't come equipped with barf bags.

One thing that surprised me when we got out of the Cessna to stretch our legs was how green things were.

There was real, green grass beside the tarmac. Spring had already come to Minnesota, at least this part of it. Trees had fresh, bright leaves. The UP was still bleak. Maybe that rain would bring the woods back to life.

Butch had parked her big, black Jeep SUV at the air strip. It had the lightning bolt and fist logo on the side which made me suspect she was using the vehicle as a tax write off. She drove us into the city on a freeway. It was practically a new experience for me, all those lanes of traffic. There are no freeways in the UP, just two lane roads, some with strategic passing lanes.

We checked in at the hotel. It was big, too, made me feel like a country girl. The women in the lobby were dressed to the nines. In the UP some of us had barely put away our waffle stomper boots and here were women in heels that looked like they were four inches high. I only own one pair of heels in case Charlie takes me dancing, which isn't often. My mother had pointed me to a brand of shoe called Easy Spirits, which were her choice.

I told myself I wasn't in Minnesota to make a fashion statement. With me, what you see is what you get. I stood back, clutching my laptop in its case and the WMUP video camera like it was a life preserver. I felt conspicuous, out of my depth.

I wished Charlie had come along, but that wasn't possible. With him, this might have been fun. To be honest, except for that trip to Orlando, this was the first time I was out of the UP. Minneapolis wasn't exactly a foreign country, but it was not my turf, hey.

The reservation put me in an adjoining room with my so-called bodyguards next door. Imogene's lawyer, Mr. Saunders, had warned me about being influenced by the warriors. When Butch Wallace told me to just put meals or the bar tab on the room bill, I just nodded. I wasn't going to do that. No way. I'd charge the meals on my Visa card and see who'd reimburse me, Saunders or the Network. I didn't want to be beholden to Imogene, either. I just hoped Mr. Krakow would come through.

Though I had my press credential from WMUP, since I was embedded, as Queen Annie put it, it would be nicer if I was official NBC. Nobody in Minnesota would know who or what the hell WMUP was, maybe some 10 watt local FM station or, worse yet, the Chinook Winds Casino. That carried zero status in the broadcast business.

Before meeting everyone for dinner, I booted up my laptop and logged on using the free Wi-Fi to check the email. I phoned my folks, Queen Annie, and Charlie to say I'd arrived OK and was waiting in suspense to find out what was next on the agenda.

Chapter Thirty-six: Klaus von Seuler

Butch Wallace said hotel restaurants weren't very nice. She had something special in mind, a Lebanese place. Glennie said she was vegan. Masha wanted meat. I wanted out.

I needed some private time away from my keepers. They had their stories to tell, their private jokes, and I felt out of place, like the unwelcome guest. Were they suspicious of me as a TV reporter, or glad for the potential publicity?

I suspect they felt I was pretty boring. I'm not the life of the party. I know a few Yooper jokes, but if you're not from the UP they're just obscure and dumb. At the Mather brunch I had just sat and listened, not contributing to the conversation, and trying to remember details without actually taking out my pocket notebook to write down notes. They must have thought I was pretty dull.

I got a table for one in the hotel dining room. I think I must have been a little airsick. It might have been the stress of riding through the turbulence and coming in for a landing. I ordered something simple, soup and salad, and was shocked at the big city prices.

When the food arrived I just sat there for a minute staring at it like it was something foreign and unfamiliar.

Before I could pick up my soup spoon I was interrupted.

It was a good looking guy in a yellow jacket with a foreign cut. He had a blonde mustache and a polite manner. I thought I'd seen him sort of lurking when we checked in and thinking that maybe he was one of G. Wallace's FBI guys. It was a thought I had dismissed because he looked foreign.

"Excuse me. You are from WMUP." He pointed to the video camera I had brought with me like a security blanket.

"Yes."

"You are here for the StopRape trial?"

Not knowing the right answer, that I was a subpoenaed witness or a journalist from the network, I answered with a question, "How did you guess?"

"I saw you come in zat car with the Women Warrior logo on it."

Well, that figured. So why was he interested? Maybe he was FBI after all.

He pulled a chair from an adjoining table, sat down, and introduced himself. "Klaus von Seuler. I'm here for *Der Spiegel.*"

"I'm Kerstin Mikkola."

„Ach! Zatt Kerstin Mikkola!"

My God, he knew all about me. The U-Tube video must have gone viral.

I had to divert him. I didn't want to admit my mistake in giving Imogene the DVD of the unedited interview, the hate mail that followed and all that. I didn't want my stupidity spread over the pages of *Der Spiegel.* "I hear that there's a German equivalent of the StopRape web site." I knew that much but not the details.

"Zere is."

He had a little lisp. I guess Germans have trouble with their th's. "Do the Germans also have their Woman Warriors?"

"Somezing like zat. The government is nervous about zem. Zey are afraid of another Bader Meinhof."

I didn't know Bader Meinhof. "Who are they?"

"Zey were a gang of anti-government anarchists or Moists. Zey were violent, robbed banks, made bombs."

"The Women Warriors aren't anti government," I explained. "They're vigilantes out to harass alleged rapists and registered sex offenders." I didn't want to go into the Sauvenier case. How would I explain to a strange, foreign visitor that Sgt. Sauvenier had been castrated and his testicles nailed to the doorpost? It wasn't a subject to go with my soup and salad.

"Who were the women you came mit...er, with?" He obviously guessed that and wanted confirmation.

"Women Warriors. They're my self-appointed bodyguards. It's kind of a joke." I tried to laugh it off, but I was in earnest. Butch Wallace, Masha and Glennie were too intense for me to be comfortable around them. I considered myself lucky to have escaped long enough to get dinner on my own. I also guessed that they'd seen enough of me for the time being.

Von Seuler's eyebrows went up. "Why bodyguards?"

I admitted, "I'm also called as an expert witness." The subpoena hadn't used that term. I made it up so sound more important.

I was stuck after all. Maybe if I told him what he wanted to know he'd go away. While my soup got cold I explained that it all started when I interviewed Imogene Michener about her assault and the StopRape web site. I didn't tell him about my giving her the DVD. I did say that because it was only my face that appeared on U-Tube people thought I was part of her program.

To my dismay, Klaus von Seuler was taking notes, making a pest of himself. He wanted to know all about me, about my job, about the TV station. He was thorough, and wrote everything down. I asked, "What do you need all this for? I suppose you want to know about the trial, not me."

He smiled and stroked his little mustache, like maybe it was a new one and he wasn't yet used to it. "Ze story of Kerstin Mikkola is a good one for *Die Deutsche Frau.*"

"What's that?" I almost said "Zat," picking upon his funny accent.

"A woman's magazine. Gossip, personalities, recipes."

I could see he'd cash in on his *Spiegel* trip with a little story on the side. "Oh."

Like a magician he produced a little digital camera. "You mind if I take a photo?"

It was bad enough that he invited himself to my table for one. Now he wanted my picture, too, as if I were some sort of celebrity and he were paparazzi. At least I'd had my hair done. I could have said no, but I knew he could sneak one, and I admit I was flattered. "You should get pictures of Imogene Michener, not me. She's the one being sued."

"Is she here at ze hotel?"

"I don't know." I didn't even know if she would be appearing in court. She didn't have to, if this was a preliminary moment like Saunders planned. At least my job was conveniently located at the old airport. Imogene was in Rock, for Pete's sake. I hadn't thought about her having to travel to Minneapolis. She'd have to drive to Marquette, then fly to Chicago and get a plane to the Twin Cities. It would take all day. I was lucky to get that ride from Wallace, even if it did scare the heck out of me.

Von Seuler snapped several pictures and I tried not to pose. I just wanted him to go away. I gestured helplessly at my food and he got the hint.

The German got up, gave me a continental bow, and apologized. "Sorry. I am keeping you from your meal. If you'd like I can buy you a drink after. Seven-thirty in ze hotel bar?"

I wished he would just go away, but I wanted to ask him about his job at *Der Spiegel* and what was going on in Germany with their version of StopRape, so I agreed.

The more I thought about it, the more certain I was that this von Seuler was not sent by *Der Spiegel*. He was probably a free lance, speculating, which would be why he wanted to sell something to the *Deutsche Frau*, too. What kind of magazine was that? Something like *Woman's Day*?

I was right. It was the first thing I asked him when I met him at the bar. He was a freelance, took a chance that the German magazine would pay his expenses. He had taken a train from Hamburg to Amsterdam and a charter flight from Schlipol, a direct flight from there to Minneapolis.

Von Seuler wanted to buy me a drink, but I turned down that offer. A beer is more my speed. I'd pay with my own cash, while it lasted. It was the most expensive glass of beer I'd ever had, so I was going to nurse it.

Von Seuler had friends at the German magazine and was sure he'd get a good price for an exclusive.

Mr. Saunders was at the bar, too, came up to me and asked me to join him at a table. Without invitation, von Seuler tagged along as if I were his date or something.

Saunders had a table with an attractive woman about my age. He introduced me as Kerstin Mikkola, but I added "I'm from WMUP television," and showed my camera with its station ID sticker. I introduced Klaus von Seuler as a reporter sent by *Der Spiegel*. I winked at von Seuler, who appreciated my official sounding introduction.

The woman with Saunders turned out to be Reva Katz. She had black hair with a white streak that might be a sign of early aging or an affectation done by her hair dresser. She wore a shiny blouse and a glittery necklace with matching earrings.

"So you're representing the Women Warriors," I said. I wondered if the two lawyers saw themselves as associates or adversaries. Both parties were being sued by the same consortium in the class action against StopRape.com and the Women Warriors as if the two were conjoined. I knew they weren't. I thought maybe that would save the plaintiffs money, killing two birds with one stone as they say.

We were to be in court Monday morning at ten o'clock. I asked, "Is Imogene Michener here, too?"

Saunders made a glum face. "I'm afraid not. She's had a relapse of her PTSD. The thought of appearing gave her a panic attack. I told her it wasn't necessary for her to be here."

I remembered how reluctant Imogene was to show her face at the first interview. Later, when I saw her in her own home she wasn't so intimidated. I didn't realize how fragile someone like that could be. Of course Sauvenier wasn't going to be there. The likelihood was that she had never actually met the opposing parties. They were just faces on the web page. I doubted that she'd even met any of the Women Warriors.

If it weren't that it was a class action suit, each of the men accused of being rapists or molesters would have to sue individually. Then the women who denounced them would have to appear, too. From what I had seen on the StopRape site, that could be hundreds of individual cases, literally. No wonder many victims would rather drop a rape case than have to face their accuser and publicly relate all the gory details. Telling their stories on the StopRape.com web page wasn't anonymous, but it wasn't face to face. People will say a lot on the internet that they'd hesitate to say in public. Of course, the internet is public. That's the danger.

I was tactful enough not to mention that Saunders had already told me his tactical plans. That was in confidence.

Klaus von Seuler sat taking notes as fast as he could, which intimidated the lawyers. Saunders wasn't going to stand for it. He reached across the table and put his hand on top of von Seuler's, stopping his pen. "Do you mind? This is a private meeting."

Embarrassed, von Seuler put away his pen and got up to leave. "Excuse me." He made a little bow and retreated, but he stayed within sight.

I suspected he was using that little camera for some photographs of us.

Saunders got up, too and took me by the am out of earshot of the other lawyer. Speaking softly he warned, "Be careful of Butch Wallace and her pals. You understand, Imogene Michener is not doing anything illegal. I wouldn't say that about the Warriors."

I told him about the map Glennie had and the pictures Masha took of the homes of the registered sex offenders.

Saunders shook his head, obviously worried. "All the more reason to keep your distance. When the police do that, it's official investigative business. When the unofficial Women Warriors do it, it's stalking. You understand?"

I nodded. I could see that the Warriors saw themselves as a sort of neighborhood watch. At what point did they go over the line to harassment? If course, it was their intention to intimidate and even frighten the men who were accused of rape. That was probably the reason for the class action suit against them.

I didn't know if intimidation was what a lawyer would call actionable. Certainly assault was. Whoever castrated Sauvenier could go to prison, but that was in California. Butch Wallace was from Minnesota. At least, that was the license plate on her SUV.

I didn't mention the aborted run back in the woods to find Joe Pascoe's place.

"They're going to want to use you as a witness to prove what they do is harmless and legitimate."

I agreed. "They think they're doing a public service."

Saunders almost laughed. "Your friendly neighborhood watch."

We returned to the table. From Saunders' forced cordiality it was clear to me that he was playing it cool with Reva Katz. She might have wanted Saunders to agree they were both defending against the class action suit, that they were on the same side. She hadn't met the lawyers for the opposition, but she said she had read the brief they'd submitted to the court.

A brief? That was something I hadn't seen. As a spectator reporting on a couple of court cases before, Native American stuff when I was a broadcaster for the Casino, I hadn't been on the inside. I didn't know about briefs or case law. The closest I'd got to legal stuff in college was some lectures about libel and copyright infringement.

Of course, hanging out with Charlie I was exposed to the cop's side of things, about the Miranda rule, stuff like that, but, hey, not what actually went on behind the scenes in a law suit.

Saunders explained that because American law is built on precedents, each side gathers up examples from previous cases to justify their own point of view. I realized, from our previous conversation about splitting the case, Saunders' brief would be radically different from Katz's.

Both sides were concerned with defamation, which was the claim of the class action suit. Imogene Michener didn't defame anyone with the StopRape.com website. If the guys whose pictures and accusations were posted on the site felt they were being defamed, libeled, slandered, or whatever, that was on the heads of the people, mostly women, who posted the accusations, not Imogene Michener.

I remembered the fine print in the contract. When someone joined and paid for the right to post something they paid the five dollar fee and accepted full responsibility for the content and absolved StopRape of any liability. It was sort of like buying space in the newspaper for a classified ad. I wondered if that would stand up in court.

Saunders said he could send me a PDF file of the brief he'd submitted to the court, but it was a couple of hundred pages, and we were to be in court the next day. There wouldn't be time.

Reva Katz had little to say. She was serious and up tight. I suspected she'd need several drinks to loosen up. I wasn't going to stick around that long. I sensed the tension between the two lawyers, their professional congeniality masking an innate hostility, like a couple of boxers circling the ring before the first punch was thrown.

I rejoined von Seuler at the bar and asked him his opinion. I realized that reporters pick each other's brains and share information. With him writing for a German publication, we were not in competition. What I really wanted to know was something about the German version of the StopRape web site. He was well informed. I don't know German, except they make big words out of a lot of little ones strung together, which made the name of the German site unintelligible to me.

The result was basically the same, except there were differences in German law. Von Seuler explained that if rapists were a race or a religion they'd be protected by the anti-hatred laws that resulted from the Holocaust. Rapists, of course, could be anybody, men or women, and their victims of either gender. But libel was still libel.

I remembered from my class on libel that the best defense was the truth. As long as you didn't tell lies, you'd avoid losing a libel suit. But unless the men whose pictures were posted had actually been convicted, these were allegations. That's why we at WMUP always used the word "alleged" even if a killer were caught with the smoking gun in his hand.

My advantage was that I was the only one outside of Saunders who knew Imogene Michener's story personally. She'd told me everything before I did the initial broadcast interview, and I had visited her home in Rock. Of course, I only heard her side of the rape story. Sauvenier was dead.

That explained why Saunders wanted me there. As a character witness I could back up Imogene if she wasn't present. I'd be more than willing to do that.

What I did learn from my conversation with von Seuler was that this was very much an international story. Otherwise *Der Spiegel* would not be interested. That was important, too, for the network. Sasha Krakow would want to know that. I still hadn't heard back from him.

It was too late to call, since Krakow's office was in Chicago and offices were closed. I retreated to the neutral ground of my hotel room to boot up the new laptop, take notes, and send him an email, backed up as usual on my flash drive which I keep in my purse.

This was a nasty business, and I was in the thick of it. Wallace might think she owned me, but she would be disappointed. I was a reporter, not a spokes person. The fourth estate has to be objective.

I wondered how the court case would pan out.

Chapter Thirty-seven: Summary judgment?

The breakfast at the hotel included about everything you'd want: bacon, sausage, scrambled eggs, cold cereal, juice, do it yourself waffles, even some stewed prunes for the constipated traveler. I was caught between my appetite and my need to control my weight. In front of a TV camera you look twenty pounds heavier. I didn't need that.

Before the Women Warriors could grab me for a ride to the court in Wallace's Jeep SUV, Saunders spirited me away. He drove a Prius hybrid, something I'd never ridden in before. I was so taken by the built in GPS screen that I missed seeing the actual scenery as we drove to the court.

The courtroom was impressive. The architecture is intended to have a psychological effect on all present. The judge's bench is elevated like a throne. Spectators are at a distance, and a uniformed bailiff adds another measure of authority. The intention is to make the lawyers and their clients feel small in front of all that authority. My own role was ambiguous—witness of what? And reporter for whom? For Queen Annie and WMUP of courts, and the network, I hoped.

We would be appearing in front of a judge, no jury, as this was preliminary. The judge was a woman about sixty, with frizzy grey hair. She wore a black robe and a tired expression that told me she had seen it all and was tired of it. This was not a fiery Judge Judy looking for a fight like on TV.

When she saw I'd brought a video camera, she wouldn't allow it. Queen Annie would be disappointed. I'd have to fall back on front step interviews with the various parties. I could do that.

Lawyers Saunders and Katz sat at the same table with their briefcases and papers. Behind them, a couple of seats away, I saw Butch Wallace, Masha and Glennie, the gang of three. I had my laptop so I could take notes.

I saw Klaus von Seuler at the back of the room, but no other members of the press. I thought that was odd, that if the case could attract someone to come all the way from Germany, it should be noticed by a local newspaper reporter. Maybe my involvement with the case made it seem more important than it actually was to the rest of the world. Of course, civil suits don't attract the same attention as gruesome murder cases or major celebrities like a Woody Allen child custody case.

The opposition was at the other side of the room. This was the first I'd seen the lawyer, or lawyers for the plaintiffs. They were two men in three piece suits and ties that looked expensive. By that I mean expensive per billable hour.

Sitting with them was an older man, not as formal in his clothing, no necktie, but with an aura that spelled money, the kind of a man who was rich enough to come to the office in his jogging sweats. If I had a photographic memory I might have identified him from the many faces posted on the StopRape web site, but there were too many of those. I guessed one of the alleged victims had accused someone powerful with enough money to organize a class action suit and raise righteous indignity to new heights.

Klaus von Seuler saw me and nodded with a smile. He was taking notes like mad and probably sneaking photos. Nowadays with cell phones capable of making videos, there was no limit to what could be done unobtrusively.

Saunders, looking over the tops of his reading glasses like Carl Levin, Michigan's senior senator, spoke only to the judge.

"I wish to file a claim for a summary dismissal. The plaintiff's suit is frivolous. It has no substance."

Saunders had explained to me that a summary dismissal could throw the whole case out of court. It was the cheapest and safest escape, no actual trial.

The other lawyers objected strenuously.

The judge sighed and rapped her gavel. "Denied. Let's get on with it." Clearly she thought this was all a waste of her time.

The plaintiff leaned back in his chair, his arms crossed, and smirked. I asked Saunders who the man was and he whispered, "Howard Rickenbacker. He's a millionaire developer. A real estate agent claimed he raped her, but he can afford high priced lawyers and got off."

But he didn't escape being publicly denounced on the web site. How many of the alleged rapists had a similar beef?

Saunders had to fall back to plan B. "Your honor, we have two cases here which are improperly bundled. One is a case of defamation and libel. Imogene Michener has not defamed or libeled anyone. The StopRape.com web site is only a vehicle for others to use. I draw your attention to the contract signed by everyone who posts to the site. This is a freedom of speech, first amendment case, a matter of interpretation of the Constitution. Imogene Michener is no more liable than the movie house that shows a film some people find offensive. I request a change of venue. As this is a constitutional issue of first amendment Freedom of Speech it should be tried in a Federal Court."

A change of venue would get the case off the docket of the tired judge we were appearing before. It was a smart move, the courts being so overloaded. Moving the case to a backed up Federal court would postpone action for months, if not years.

"I'll take that under advisement," the judge said.

What was she going to do? Retire to her chambers and mull over it for a few weeks? I was certainly not going to hang around Minneapolis waiting for another court date. I had to go back to the UP and my job, if it was still there.

It was becoming clear to me that the drama in real court scenes was quiet, couched in the formal language of legal argument, lawyer versus lawyer, not like a dramatic Perry Mason episode on television. This was not television.

Hey, I was television, "Kerstin Mikkola, girl reporter!" You could almost make a soap opera of my life, except there wasn't enough excitement in covering a bear on someone's back porch to justify the expense of an ad for Kibbles and Bits.

Mr. Saunders turned to me and shook my hand. "Looks like you can go home, Miss Mikkola, at least for the time being."

I wasn't sure I was ready to bail out. Why call me as a witness unless it was to be assured of television news time? Butch Wallace wanted me in her corner. Saunders wanted me, too. I wanted no personal involvement in either side. As a TV reporter, this was my story. I'd stick it out.

I have to admit, my objectivity was getting pretty thin. I sympathized with Imogene. She was the victim. She was the person who, in spite of debilitating PTSD that got her a medical discharge from the Marines, had the courage and guts to do that web site. Good for her!

The Women Warriors were a different story. I didn't know who put the BITCH sticker on my Taurus, but I wouldn't want one that said RAPIST on my car, either, especially if it was a he said/she said case of consensual sex that went wrong, like happened with Joe Pascoe and Heather Rasmussen. I wouldn't want a bunch of hell raising warriors tearing up my lawn with their hog Harleys, if I had a lawn. Which I don't.

I was reminded of that quotation, "When Law and Order fail, the only option is revenge." Well, here I was in court hoping that the law would prevail.

I'd put those questions to Butch Wallace in front of my camera. I could see a confrontation coming.

Chapter thirty-eight: Retreat to the UP

When the judge broke for lunch, I managed to get all the principals out on the courthouse steps for some on camera face time. What I was hoping for, and got, was to catch Wallace and the plaintiff, that real estate millionaire Rickenbacker, in an argument. For a moment I was afraid Butch was going to punch the man in the face, but at the last second she realized she was on camera and didn't want that kind of evidence of assault broadcast on the six o'clock.

Rickenbacker and his lawyers retreated to wherever they were having lunch. Wallace and her girls were going somewhere else, thankfully, or there might be a food fight. For the sake of retaining my objectivity, I declined her invitation.

My videotaping of Butch Wallace got heated, too. Finally, she demanded, "Whose side are you on, Mikkola?"

So now it was Mikkola, not Kerstin. "I'm not anyone's side. I report the news. I don't make it."

She was steaming mad. "You ungrateful bitch."

I turned off the camera. "Well, thanks for the ride, anyway, and the hotel room. That doesn't mean you own me or WMUP."

"Well, I hope you find your own way back to your crappy, old motel in Yooperland."

That ended it. Saunders had reminded me that so far as he was concerned, I was free to go. Butch Wallace wasn't going to give me a free air taxi service return to the UP. When I told him I'd have to fly back to Michigan on my own tab, he mumbled something evasive, like he'd get back to me. Like in my dreams, hey. I could see my credit card statement climbing. As small compensation Saunders offered me a lift back to the hotel.

True to his form, Klaus von Seuler imposed himself on us and got a ride, too. He sat in the back seat of the Prius quiet as you please. Though I found him pushy at times, I had to admire his persistence. As a freelance, self-employed, he had to be aggressive to get his stories. We Yoopers are more laid back. Maybe it's the long winters that lull us into a state of semi-hibernation.

When we got to the hotel he sidled up to me. "You wish to share some notes?"

I told him, "You betcha" which confused him because he didn't talk Yooper. We had lunch in the hotel restaurant to recapitulate the morning session. I hadn't checked out and just for spite invited von Seuler to lunch on my—Butch Wallace's—tab. We exchanged cell phone numbers and email addresses.

Being away from home, I was getting antsy. I didn't want to try Queen Annie's patience by being away too long. There was Larry Pelenpaa who would be glad, I was sure, to keep my slot on the news broadcasts.

I had enough information for a good story. I was thinking beyond a two minute sound bite on the ten o'clock. This was worth a half hour show, maybe more, and a potential one hour special on the network. We could piece together some of the old footage, screen shots from the web site, including the accusation against Mr. Rickenbacker. Grab his face off the StopRape web site, then switch to the footage I took on the court house steps. I could easily put together the twenty minutes left of a half hour show, plus the obligatory ten minutes of commercials.

At this point I also wanted to get away from Minneapolis and especially Butch Wallace and her gang. Then I had to arrange a flight back to Michigan.

Back in my hotel room I booted up the laptop and looked for a cheap fare. American had a flight leaving at 3:30 with a layover in Chicago, arriving at K.I. Sawyer at 8:15. All connections arrived in Marquette at the same time. It's not like there are many flights to the UP. There were other possibilities from Minneapolis, but this was the fewest hours en route and the shortest layover at O'Hare. It was going to cost almost three hundred bucks, one way. Ouch.

Saunders never actually agreed to cover my expenses. That was a big disappointment. When you book a ticket long in advance, you sometimes can get a good rate. Last minute bookings are the most expensive.

I phoned Queen Annie and said I was on my way back, but would have to fly commercial. She said I should show her the bill when I got in. She didn't say she'd pay for it or even a portion. Heck, I was just flying from Minnesota to Michigan. It wasn't like I was von Seuler coming all the way from Germany on spec.

My last hope was to call Sasha Krakow at the network. I gave him a detailed verbal report and promised some good interview footage with the principals. He had hoped Imogene would be there, too, but I told him she'd had a relapse of her PTSD and couldn't face up to it. I could imagine the flashback when she'd be in court instead of before a commanding officer who just blew her off. It would bring back all the old agony.

Just to make the story more attractive, I told Krakow that *Der Spiegel* had sent a reporter all the way from Hamburg, Germany, which technically wasn't true.

To my huge relief, Krakow agreed. Even better, he said the network had a standing account with the airline. He gave me the essential information to give to a ticket agent for a free ticket home. Wow. What a difference between my small town penny pinching and the big time!

Trouble was, the 3:30 was the last flight of the day to make the connection to Michigan. I might just make it.

I packed. While I waited in the lobby for the shuttle to the airport I called Saunders on my cell phone. He was at the court, and hugely relieved that the judge agreed to split the suits. Imogene's case would be reduced to a First Amendment freedom of speech issue. The Women Warriors were not part of it. Whether the class action suit would stand up against the allegers as a group was debatable. Individuals would have to sue on their own, a case by case basis. That would kill it.

The case against the Women Warriors as a national organized group for harassment, vandalism, and certainly castration of an alleged rapist were criminal matters, not a civil suit, and were up to individual police departments to pursue.

In the meantime, I knew G. Marshall and the rest of the FBI were watching and waiting for some actionable interstate conspiracy. The irony was, who had more rights? The accused rapists or their victims?

Mr. Rickenbacker had wasted his money. If he sued the real estate agent she might not have any money he could collect for damages. Was he willing to testify and give a blow by blow description of his side of the alleged assault? Did he want his face in the papers as an accused rapist? Probably not.

I was looking forward to getting back to the UP to edit the recordings I'd made and piece together the story for Queen Annie and the network. Maybe this would be my ticket to big time.

If it were only that simple.

I nervously approached the American airlines ticket counter. I had no reservation, but I had Krakow's company account information. There were no seats available in coach. Darn. I was so stressed out I nearly cried from frustration. The agent took pity on me. She was impressed with my press credentials. They could put me in first class as far as Chicago.

I tried to act like it was just the way we do it when we work for the network. I felt like a celebrity. Well, maybe not a real one but I could pretend. Beyond Chicago there was no such thing as a first class seat to the UP. Those were little planes.

Golly. First class! It was a big step up from that awful jumbo jet flight to Orlando. Seated in comfort, I was able to boot up the laptop and start the outline for a half hour show. They even served a snack and wine, no extra charge. I felt spoiled. I could get used to this, but not yet.

The flight to O'Hare in Chicago landed at terminal three, same terminal as the feeder flight to K.I. Sawyer, but still a long haul dragging my carry-on, the laptop in its case, and the WMUP camera to the gate.

I just made it in time to board and before takeoff called Charlie to say I was arriving at 8:15 and could he pick me up? Sure. He wanted to know all about the trial and those Women Warriors.

My glimpse into the cockpit of the feeder plane didn't give me much confidence in the crew. The pilot was a young guy. At least the co-pilot was a woman. Those feeder airlines pay pilots less than K-12 school teachers. The difference is if a third grade teacher makes a mistake, she doesn't crash the school and kill a classroom full of kids.

We almost didn't land. There was fog, typical at that time of year, and we circled the field a couple of times before the pilot had the courage to land.

What a relief. I was glad to be back in the UP. There were still puddles on the tarmac when we deplaned. Somewhere in the foggy night the peeper frogs were still singing their love songs. The Lake Superior air was a pleasure to breathe again after the diesel exhaust and pollution of Minneapolis.

Charlie pulled the sheriff's patrol car right up to the plane. I guess it looked like he might be receiving a prisoner. To tell the truth, I felt reprieved. It was all over but the shouting, I thought.

I was mistaken. I remembered Heather Rasmussen. She lived right on the old B52 K.I Sawyer airbase in one of those homes for the military. I suggested, "Let's check in on Rasmussen."

Having installed the dead bolt on her door, Charlie knew the house.

Heather was suspicious when we knocked. She came to the door in slacks and a blouse she was hastily buttoning. She was glad to see me again, not glad enough to invite me and Charlie inside. Obviously, we had interrupted something.

"I was in Minneapolis for the law suit," I explained. "Just got back. It's a long story, but I wanted to ask you. Did you take Joe Pascoe's picture down from the StopRape website?"

I think she was a little drunk. She looked guilty and apologized. "Gee, I forgot, hey."

"Will you remember to please take it down?"

She promised.

I shook my head at Charlie, who was also sure she would forget. As I turned to go I asked, "Are you still seeing Joe Pascoe?"

"Not since he got out of jail. He's still mad at me."

"So he's out?"

"Yesterday."

It sounded like their little love affair was over. I didn't think it meant much to Heather anyway. It reminded me of my own relationship with Charlie. How much did he mean to me? He's a good man, but like I said before, I could never marry a cop. You'd never know what will happen. With thousands of gun nuts wanting carry permits, even a routine traffic stop can turn deadly. A policeman's most dangerous encounters are in calls about domestic disputes. Try to get people to calm down and get shot for being a good Samaritan. I couldn't live with that.

We had a lot to talk about while Charlie drove me back to WMUP to check in and pick up my car. After all the stress of travel I needed a cuddle, but he had to go back on the lookout for drunk drivers and the like.

They didn't expect me to be back for the ten o'clock broadcast. Larry Pelenpaa was going over the notes with the floor manager and Sarah. From the way they looked at each other I suspected there might be something more going on between them than a weather report.

Queen Annie wasn't there, of course. I'd see her the next afternoon.

When I drove up to my place at the old motel the motion activated lights went on, the brightness spilling over to the unit next door. There were three Harley hogs parked outside. The UP is not a good place for someone who wants to own a big Harley. With snow on the ground half the year, a motorcycle isn't much good. Not many people up here can afford what, thirty or forty thousand for a road toy? This is a part of the world where the used car dealers get the dregs at the auctions. So who were they?

Before I went inside my place I checked the license plates. Two of the bikes were registered in Illinois, one in Wisconsin. It looked like Butch Wallace had set up a local headquarters in the Women Warrior campaign against sexual predators.

Chapter thirty-nine: Joe Pascoe

I was just having breakfast when one of the neighbors knocked at the door. She was dressed in biker's leathers, a heavy jacket with lots of studs for sliding on pavement in case you fall off. She was about thirty, I guess, with rough skin and holding a map I recognized. It was the one Glennie had with the marked locations of the local registered sex offenders.

She didn't introduce herself, just assumed I knew what it was all about. Obviously she'd been briefed. She pointed to the marks on the city map. "Looking for some jerk called Pascoe."

"You won't find him on that. Doesn't live in town."

"Where is he, then?"

Deliberately evasive, I shook my head. "Can't say. Somewhere out in the woods. There's lots of forest around here. The whole UP is mostly forest, except where it's swamp."

She nodded. "And bugs."

I'd almost forgotten about the bugs. The black flies were coming out, nasty little critters with a bite that keeps on bleeding, especially around the hair line. "Better keep your helmet on," I suggested. "Don't bother about Pascoe. He's not a problem."

Normally my instinct would be to try to interview her on the spot, get her name, why she was in the UP, stuff like that, but I was intimidated and certainly not objective as I should be as a journalist. I was developing an aversion for the Women Warriors.

I practically shoved her out the door and went to the phone to call Charlie. He was on patrol. His radio signal was breaking up. "Those Women Warriors are here looking for Joe Pascoe."

Charlie got the message and knew what it was about, but he was so far away I didn't think he'd get to Pascoe's in time. I smelled a story and an opportunity, so I called WMUP. Queen Annie was having her first cup of coffee and cigar. She wanted me to tell her about the trial, but I put her off. "I'll tell you later. The Women Warrior biker gang are in town looking for sex offenders. I called the sheriff to warn them not to make any mischief. They're looking for Joe Pascoe. I'll try to get there first. No telling what they'll do if they catch him."

Of course, I new darned well what they might do. Another Sauvenier castration.

I put on my jacket with its tight hood and my Deet bug spray in the pocket, standard equipment at this time of year. I grabbed the 410 shot gun from its hiding place in the broom closet and slipped the Beretta out from under the mattress.

I had that little holster I'd bought but felt stupid wearing it even though I did have my temporary carry permit. This time I put it on, felt the heft on my hip. Would I start swaggering like some two gun cowboy in an old John Wayne movie? I looked myself in the mirror and said to myself, 'Kerstin Mikkola, what the hell are you doing?'

I didn't wait for the answer.

Outside I heard the three Harleys fire up with a roar and watched as the three Women Warriors accelerated down US41 toward town.

It was not the right direction, but I was sure they'd figure out where Pascoe was. Glennie had probably marked his two track on the county ordinance map.

I started the Taurus, glad it had those new mud and snow tires, and, feeling like the cavalry, off I went to the rescue.

I was all bluff, of course. I didn't know if those bikers were armed, and I am a terrible shot. The .410 is OK for rabbits, but not for women wearing heavy leather protective clothing and helmets with face shields. As for the Beretta, well, it might be OK for the Mossad to give two quick pops to the back of someone's head like Charlie told me. I didn't want to get that close to anybody.

I admit I was caught up in the moment. If I'd thought rationally I wouldn't have done it. It's not that I particularly like Joe Pascoe. He called me a bitch and said he'd kill me, but that was all blowing smoke. I sized him up as basically an occasionally mean drunk. Three months in the county jail would have sobered him up, I hoped. I didn't think he'd have reformed, gone on the wagon, found Jesus or anything like that. But he wasn't a rapist. Of that I was certain. He'd be no match for the Women Warriors.

I ignored the No Trespassing sign nailed to a tree near the entrance to Pascoe's drive. In the short time since I had attempted Pascoe's road with Butch Wallace and her girls, someone had been there. The muddy surface had been driven on, maybe once, not enough to break it up. The recent rain had made it worse.

Driving in mud is a little like driving in snow. You try never to spin the wheels or you dig yourself a hole you can't get out of. Gentle and easy does it, but just never stop. If you stop, well, you might not get started again.

There was one low spot and a big puddle from all that rain the day before. No telling how deep it was. You could get in, be stuck, and have to wade out. Of course, Pascoe has that high mud buggy with big wheels, raised up so you almost need a ladder to get up into the cab. Now it was clear why.

I eased the Taurus around the edge of the mud hole, made it around a little bend and there it was: Pascoe's place. His was the reason why some people call the UP the Appalachia of the North. This was the poverty privileged Americans never see.

A sign nailed to a post that had once been part of a barbed wire fence said, "Keep Out. Trespassers will be Shot. Survivors will be Shot Again." I guessed that Pascoe must be an NRA member. I remembered his rifle had been confiscated as stolen goods. Maybe he had another. Would he actually shoot a trespasser?

Would he shoot me?

I saw Pascoe's tired old truck, spattered with mud. In the yard was the carcass of an old snowmobile that must have been cannibalized for parts and abandoned. The outhouse behind the shack testified that there was no running water.

The shack had never been painted. The roof consisted of a patchwork of old shingles and tarpaper slabs. The bricks of the chimney were loose. Oddly enough there was a TV dish mounted on the side of the house, aimed at a distant satellite. Everyone has their priorities.

Instead of steps up to the platform that served as a porch there was a stack of cement blocks.

It was a sorry sight, and Pascoe fit right in. He was slumped on an old, weather-beaten couch that must have stood out there all winter. He was wearing a torn, dirty tee shirt, jeans without knees, and an expression of hopeless despair. When he saw me drive up he dropped his beer can. It joined its empty mates at his feet, his first six pack of the day.

He looked up as I opened the door to the Taurus and stepped down into the muddy yard. Then he recognized me.

"What the hell? BITCH!"

I ignored his invective. This was not about me. "Take it easy, Mr. Pascoe. I just came out to make sure you're safe."

That puzzled him. He tried to focus his eyes and understand what I was talking about. "Safe?"

"The Women Warriors biker gang are on their way."

He didn't know anything about the Women Warriors. "What for?"

"It's because Heather put your picture up on the StopRape website."

He didn't know about web sites, either. Pascoe was not computer literate. "If you're lucky they'll just come to scare you. If you're not, they may try to castrate you."

"Bull." Now he stood up, steadied himself on the arm of the old sofa. He was so drunk, even at this early hour, there was little point in explaining anything to him. If I told him about Sauvenier and Imogene Michener he wouldn't know who that was. Putting two sentences together in the same paragraph would have been beyond his comprehension.

Then I heard the roar of the motorcycles. They were not running steadily, but accelerating, slowing, roaring, that distinctive, patented Harley sound. Obviously the Women

Warriors were not used to navigating mud on their road bikes.

I quickly grabbed the .410 shotgun out of the front seat of the Taurus, climbed the unstable cement block steps, took up my position beside Pascoe and waited.

Chapter Forty: Resolution

The three motorcycles pulled up in a row in front of my car. Bikers usually keep their machines shiny and spotless, but these were now spattered with mud. It looked like one of them had fallen over, possibly in that mud hole. They're so heavy, it would probably take all three women to stand it up again. What a mess. The women, their boots muddy, dismounted like cowboys getting off their horses after a long day on a dusty cattle drive. They were not happy.

Obviously in their intent to harass—or worse—Joe Pascoe, they hadn't expected armed resistance. When they saw me with the shot gun they stopped.

The one who had come to my door called, "Is this Joe Pascoe?"

Pascoe was still trying to get his focus and his balance. His anger was beginning to surface. "This is private property. Can't youse read signs? No tres...passing."

Another of the women ignored the warning. "You Joe Pascoe the rapist?"

I stood my ground. "Back off." Pascoe was not my friend. He was no longer Heather's boy friend. He was a sorry drunk. "He's not a rapist."

The biker whose machine had apparently fallen over was muddy up to her knees. "He's on the StopRape web site," as if that gave them permission to hunt him.

"That was supposed to be taken down."

Pascoe, bewildered, looked at me for an explanation. "What?"

I assured him, "Don't worry. I'll take care of this." Then I raised my voice. "Why don't you go back to Illinois and Wisconsin or wherever you came from? This is Yooper business. We don't need any out of state vigilantes coming in to interfere."

The apparent leader looked like she was going to give me an argument when we all heard the chirp-chirp siren of the sheriff's patrol car. It was Charlie in the Crown Victoria with the Rhino bars pulling up behind my Taurus and getting out, all business and official. He looks so great in that wide brimmed hat and uniform. I love that guy.

Right behind the Victoria was the WMUP TV van. I got a glimpse of Eino getting out, adjusting the camera on his shoulder. Larry Pelenpaa, dressed in a natty, grey suit, light blue shirt and even a tie, for Pete's sake, was with him.

So now we had three vehicles lined up on that muddy two track. The WMUP truck is heavy, and I was willing to bet my souvenir Casino chips that it would be stuck, even with its four wheel drive. Which meant we would all be stuck.

Charlie's eyes widened when he saw I had the shot gun. At least I wasn't pointing it at anyone. "What's happening, Kerstin?"

"These Women Warriors have come to harass Joe Pascoe, hey." I didn't say they wanted to geld him. I didn't know if they'd go that far.

Charlie came up to Pascoe and sized him up. Charlie's body language told me he felt sympathy and disappointment for that sorry wreck of a man. "They giving you trouble, Joe?"

Pascoe pulled himself together, tried to stand straight and self righteous. "They're trespassing."

"OK." Charlie nodded and turned to the three Warriors. "Ladies? You hear that? You're trespassing on private property." He took out his notebook and walked around the motorcycles, writing down the numbers. "Illinois? Wisconsin? Well, if you've come to tour the UP, you're welcome, but if you want trouble, forget it. As for Joe Pascoe here, he's not a rapist. If you bother him I'll arrest you for stalking. Right now you're trespassing, so I suggest you just leave. Like now."

Eino was getting it all on tape for WMUP. I admit that I mugged for the camera, playing hero, even though I hadn't done anything. This was going to be great. It was a perfect fit for my feature story about StopRape.com.

I was sure Queen Annie would be pleased and the network interested. I could hardly wait to get to the studio to tell her all the news.

The three Women Warriors fired up their heavy Harleys and left. I heard their engines laboring in the mud. Eino kept the WMUP camera trained on them as they struggled out. The woods were too thick for them to avoid the two track muddy trail, and the WMUP broadcast van was pretty wide, leaving scant room on either side.

Charlie couldn't follow them out, for he was blocked by the WMUP truck. In the end, we had to call a wrecker to tow all three vehicles back out to the gravel road. That's life in the UP.

While we waited for the wrecker, this time I was the one being interviewed. I posed with the shot gun and the little Beretta on my hip like Mickey Spillane, that author of cheap misogynistic thrillers who saw himself as a model for Mike Hammer, his tough guy protagonist.

Charlie told me about that author. I think he read all those books while he was a guard at Marquette prison. Spillane's villains were often women. I wonder what he would have thought about the Women Warriors. They saw themselves as heroic defenders of abused and raped women. I was ambivalent. "Vengeance is mine, sayeth the Lord." Maybe it was just an excuse for them to go out on the road and raise hell.

Chapter forty-one: Wrap up

For the next week Queen Annie and I worked on a script and rough cut of a half hour show about StopRape.com and the Women Warriors Against Abuse. I called Klaus von Seuler for permission to use the photos he'd sneaked in the court room and for more background on the German StopRape.com equivalent web site.

We pitched the program to Sasha Krakow.

I'd hoped to be brought to Chicago to produce the show. I should have known better, of course. Something that big needed a big time director.

Queen Annie and I had spent a whole weekend putting a show together. The special was scheduled for broadcast. The network mutilated it. While Michener's U-tube clip made it look like I was the star of her show, the network barely mentioned me at all. Sheesh.

I have to admit that under the network's producer, the story got bigger. The Women Warriors had their own international influence. It was like a dam had broken, releasing a torrent of rage. Though not as well organized as the American Warriors, there were little groups of European women who fought back, not only to shame rapists, but to intimidate them. So far as I know, no German rapist got castrated, but the Sauvenier story was widely told and enough to make the point.

Though reports of rape were up, actual incidents were down. Victims were no longer afraid to speak up. They knew there were supporters out there. There is no shame in being raped, but there is plenty of shame for people who are abusive.

What startled me was that a group of Indian women in Mumbai nearly lynched several men accused of gang raping a student. Maybe the tide is turning.

I never did get to meet Sasha Krakow at the network. I did get an invitation to go on the Morning show in New

York. Imogene Michener was still too psychologically fragile to go on network television. Tied up in the fallout from the court case and a sudden withdrawal of many of the posted accusations for fear of libel suits, she was under too much pressure. She wanted no more interviews. Since I was in on Imogene Michener's story from the start I became her spokesperson by default. It wasn't a dead loss after all.

Klaus von Seuler was called, too, because he knew the German side of the StopRape story. It was a real plum for him as a free lance. He was now officially a *Spiegel* writer.

They flew me to New York the day before the Morning show. Someone from the network met me at Kennedy in an official car. They put me up in a hotel room the Network keeps under contract with the Essex Hotel for such visitors. It's across the street from Central Park.

The trip to New York City was a whirlwind visit. I had had never seen so many people in one place, not even when I covered a hockey game. My God, but New York is crowded. I never had acrophobia and don't know the technical word for fear of crowds, but I had it.

Those New Yorkers! Always in a hurry. Rude and aggressive, they push you aside, don't make eye contact. I could never live there.

The network located von Seuler as well. While I had retreated to the UP he'd sucked up to the Women Warriors and picked their brains for hard information about their international organization. So we were both at the Essex and compared notes. It's a big story, bigger than the Morning show.

We had to be at the network offices at 5 o'clock in the morning. In spite of the early hour, I thought I looked pretty good in the power outfit my Mom and I picked out for the Minneapolis trip. I wore my only pair of heels.

When I got to the studio the women on the show looked at me like I'd crawled out from under a rock. Obviously the suit and shoes weren't up to their standard, but heck, they have all those Park Avenue stores to shop in and big salaries to make that possible. They handed me over to makeup and I was groomed for about an hour like some dog going on for the pedigree show. When the artist was done with my face and hair I hardly recognized myself in the mirror.

I'm not so dumb that I didn't catch the condescending and patronizing attitude of the people at the Network. On camera and off they did a lot of chatting and giggling. Of course, that show is what we call infotainment. It's not real news.

I'd thought that for once in my life I'd be an actual celebrity. Instead I was just a curiosity. It didn't help that they knew I'd once worked at the Chinook Winds Casino. I think they thought I was an Indian who spends weekends beating on a tom tom.

I was tempted to play the yokel game with them, talk Finn, like we go sauna, hey, but I didn't want to belittle myself or the Finns. They didn't even know how to pronounce Kerstin or Mikkola. They thought my name rhymed with Rikola, the Swiss cough drop.

I have to admit that von Seuler fared a little better. It might be his heavy German accent or his cute mustache. One of the women flirted with him. His ego swelled. Not that von Seuler needs much pumping up.

At least the film clip they showed was serious. The pictures of me standing guard to save Joe Pascoe's balls filled the TV hosts with feigned awe and admiration. I also detected a measure of aversion in their attitude toward the UP. To New Yorkers, everything west of the Hudson River is Indian Territory. That I had worked at the Chinook Winds casino only reinforced that impression. I couldn't wait to get out of there.

Well, I'd had my five minutes of fame. I got my story on the Network. I'd spent some time with the Big Girls. Wouldn't you know it, though they covered all the expenses of that New York City adventure, I didn't get paid a dime.

Someone else got the byline. I flew first class back to the Midwest, another unpleasant layover at O'Hare, and the 8:30 PM return to the old K.I. Sawyer airbase. This time there was no fog. The woods were bursting with all shades of green. The steelhead were running in the streams. Charlie picked me up in the patrol car and stayed overnight at my place. I was glad to be back in the U.P.

As for StopRape.com and the international Women Warriors story, this was only the beginning. In this business, there are always more stories. Imogene Michener is the real hero. She's going to be remembered as the Mother Theresa protector of victims of rape and abuse, the one who started a world wide movement.

As for me, I'm just Kerstin Mikkola of WMUP television in Marquette, Michigan, a small branch of the Fourth Estate. Tune in again tomorrow. Goodnight.

The end

About the author:

Though born in Chicago and raised in Indiana, Harley L. Sachs considers himself an international, having lived in Germany, Sweden, Scotland, and Denmark. He earned a degree in English at Indiana University, then served in the US Army in Germany. After getting his Master's degree at I.U. he returned to Europe and worked under cover for several years. He met and married Ulla in Stockholm, Sweden and they spent a year's honeymoon in a Scottish castle. Returning to the USA, Sachs taught English briefly at Southern Illinois University then moved to Michigan Technological University in the Upper Peninsula where he and his wife raised three daughters. He took early retirement and now lives in Portland, Oregon.

Harley L. Sachs is the author of many novels, short stories, magazine articles and newspaper columns. His short stories have been broadcast on the BBC World Service short wave and on Oregon Public Radio's Golden Hours.

If you enjoyed this Upper Peninsula of Michigan story, you may be interested in another: *Burnt Out.* Here's a sample chapter:

Chapter One

My name is Irwin Glass. I'm like the guy who wanders unwittingly into a gay biker bar by mistake and gets beat up. I don't look for trouble; it finds me. I started out as an unsuspecting kid from South Bend, Indiana, son of a k-12 teacher of social studies and history. I'm also the grandson or maybe great-grandson of someone named Isaac Melamed whose letter turned up in our attic in an envelope with an indecipherable postmark and no stamp. When I showed the letter to my dad he said he couldn't read it, but it looked like Russian. "It's a piece of history," he said, naturally, since he taught the subject. "Why don't you find out what it says? It's what we call a primary source. Old letters can be windows into the past. Maybe your past, Irwin."

So how could a Russian letter be part of my past? I got hooked on that mysterious letter. Nobody in our household could read it. You know how kids are with mysteries and secrets.

My Dad said when he was a kid you could send in a cereal box top and a dime and get a secret decoder ring and unlock the message dictated at the end of the Little Orphan Annie radio broadcast. Turned out the message was "Drink more Ovaltine."

Impressions we get at age ten can stick with us all our lives. With me it was that letter. The Melamed letter wasn't in code. It was just Russian in Cyrillic. I just had to find out what was in it, like one of those puzzles you turn around and twist and tinker with until you get the solution. There was no box top and ten cent solution.

The Melamed letter set me on a path to a world beyond South Bend. There were people out there who were not Hoosiers. I was determined to learn the language, which I did, and eventually got a BA in Russian at Indiana University in Bloomington. So what do you do with a degree in Russian when you live in Indiana? Not much.

My professor encouraged me to go on for a Masters in international relations and take the Foreign Service examination. All that was because of a faded piece of thin, foreign paper. When I finally could decipher the Russian letter, it turned out to be a plea from Isaac Melamed's sweetheart for a ticket so she could join him in America. Did he ever do it? Did they get together? There was no way of knowing. It was only a link in a chain; all the rest was lost in time. At least it didn't say "Drink more Ovaltine."

By the time I could read it, it no longer mattered. Following the dictates of my karma, I got a job in Moscow at the American Library as a promising, I hoped, member of the Foreign Service. At last I could use my Russian language. Thanks, grandpa Isaac Melamed.

Then everything fell apart.

My seduction was a textbook honey pot case, almost a cliché. It's too embarrassing to go into detail but the upshot was that my hopes for a government career were ruined. I had to start over, build a new career on my limited skills. All that graduate study went down the drain.

What skills did I have? I might teach Russian, but with the cold war over, nobody needed teachers of Russian. Chinese was the new thing, or maybe Arabic, neither of which I knew. I was reduced like some expatriate abroad forced to fall back on teaching his native language to foreigners, like James Joyce in Paris, only the foreign place I landed in was Michigan's Upper Peninsula, about as far from the beaten path as you can get in the United States unless you choose Alaska.

At least Portage Lake Michigan, home of Michigan Institute of Technology and the birthplace of professional hockey, was safe. There were no KGB officers lurking in the bushes, no CIA spies ready to betray me as happened before. In spite of false claims that I had been a paid Soviet agent, I was not a spy come into the cold. I was just another MA struggling to make a living at a university that grants tenure only to Ph.D.s. Hell, I figured, a job's a job even if it's not tenure track. At least an instructorship at Michigan Tech was a step up from being an adjunct at IU/PU in South Bend or part time at Southern Illinois. Could be worse.

When I met Ivy Hartshorne, my smart and sexy office mate, things got better. Ivy's the sporty type. You can tell by her walk. It exudes self-assurance and confidence, that she's happy in her own skin and knows who she is. She drives a little red Tracker with a ski rack on the roof. She taught me how to cross country ski, an appropriate outdoor sport in the Copper Country where there's snow for six months of the year. After a couple of hours on the Tech trails we'd go back to her place for hot cocoa and a cuddle. So here we are: married. We're both too mature for puppy love and too calculating to pass up an arrangement what benefits both of us.

Ivy's not foolish or desperate enough to say, heck with it, husband or no husband, "I want a baby before my clock runs out." And I'm not so testosterone driven that I pursue everything in a skirt with boobs. Ivy and I have an arrangement that suits us both. I like to call it mature love.

Everything was working out fine until that cute Russian student, Katarina Volodna Putinsky, showed up and claimed I'm her father, result of that one night stand in Moscow twenty years ago. That should be a lesson to all young men. It could happen to almost anyone. In my situation it was an international paternity case. An additional surprise was that, since I am her biological father, she's a US citizen. Anyway, Katya'd gone her own way for the time being.

People in Portage Lake will find other things to gossip about besides the shoot out in our kitchen. That's past history. Most people have short memories. Ivy and I could concentrate on our new married life and the coming baby.

It was a new chapter. Instead of worrying about sinister Mafia types lurking with guns we could think about prenatal care and baby clothes. We're both teaching, Ivy her classes in German for Yoopers, me in what used to be called bone head English. In the new fall term I had three mundane sections of English for foreign students, an easy teaching schedule. Life was good. Just me and my sweetie with her baby bump as they call being pregnant these days. I could look out the window of the second floor office Ivy and I shared in the Humanities building, watch the fall colors the Copper Country is known for, and be content.

A new crop of students was milling about, meeting new people and getting to know the map of the campus. The beginning of term is an exciting time, full of suspense, like what is my professor like, will there be exams and term papers, stuff like that. For me it was getting the syllabus worked out and the lesson plans. There's nothing as bad as the professor who has no plan, walks into a classroom clueless and has to wing it. If you plan ahead you get fewer unpleasant surprises, you hope.

It was a Wednesday morning when I got a surprise visit at the office from Mr. Wilkins, the FBI guy from Marquette. I thought it was a social call, but Wilkins's style can be oblique, friendly only to a point.

Wilkins isn't your stereotypical FBI guy in dark glasses with a long coat to conceal god knows what arsenal of firearms. Wilkins is a Yooper, a lifelong resident of the Upper Peninsula, stationed in Marquette a hundred miles to the east. He has a droopy mustache and wears a tarnished brass American eagle belt buckle the size of a saucer, an old fashioned, checkered mackinaw jacket and a knit wool cap that warms his balding forehead. In the parlance of detective stories he's good cop most of the time. I like him, especially if I'm not charged with anything or being investigated for laundering Russian money or caught in a riddle of who shot Ivan the Terrible in our kitchen with a 9 mm Glock.

Wilkins was the one who pointed out to me that if Katya really was my daughter she was entitled to US citizenship. I'm still not sure that was a good thing to know. On that point I'm ambivalent.

"Oh, Mr. Wilkins," I said, putting on my friendly smile but feeling a tad uneasy. "What brings you to da Tech?"

"Da Tech" is the local abbreviation for Michigan Institute of Technology.

"Thought I'd check up on you." Wilkins's tone was friendly, almost joking, the kind of tease meant to disarm and rattle at the same time.

"Katya's out in Oregon, if you're looking for her."

It wasn't that. Wilkins paused, waiting for me to confess, I suppose.

I was compelled to say something. "You're not wondering if I'm laundering Mafia money? That's settled."

"Nothing like that." He almost said "dat," the local Yooper dialect.

"You didn't drive a hundred miles just to say hello."

Wilkins admitted, "It's a nice drive at this time of year."

We call it color season in the UP. Forty different species of trees make for a glorious kaleidoscope of autumn leaves.

Wilkins closed my office door, sat down in the guest chair and unbuttoned his red and black Mackinaw jacket. I glimpsed his ever present shoulder holster. "I could use your help in something. Nothing major. Just a courtesy."

That did not sound innocent. "If you're trying to recruit me, I don't do stakeouts or stuff like that. You know how I am with guns."

"Mildly incompetent," he affirmed.

"Don't rub it in."

He got to the point at last. "I see that you've got three sections of English for foreign students."

"That's right. You must have read the catalog." Michigan Tech has over a thousand foreign students and they come from about a hundred countries, most in need of engineers so the graduates can go home and whip our butts making things we used to while Americans are reduced to service jobs like burger flipping at MacDonald's. While our local kids are getting into perpetual hock with student loans the foreign students are subsidized by their governments or their rich families. The university needs the cash for tuition even if the foreign students' English is not up to speed. That's where I come in.

"What I'd like," Wilkins said, leaning forward and lowering his voice, "is a copy of your class lists."

I was reluctant. What did he want the lists for? I didn't want to know. "I'm sure you could get that from the department head, Dr. Waarala or maybe the Dean of Students."

"Waarala says it's an issue of academic freedom. What goes on in your classes is your territory."

Waarala will always fall back on the rules and regulations and let someone else stick his neck out. I guess that goes with being a Humanities department head at an engineering school where teachers of literature rank just above the janitorial staff that cleans the toilets. "There's not much left of academic freedom these days," I said. I was thinking about all the rules about discrimination, sexual harassment, non-fraternization, privacy, and so on.

"Just say it's a courtesy between friends," Wilkins said.

We are hardly friends or even colleagues. We're bound by our joint past history. Rather, I'm bound because I owe him. Wilkins knows how to lever a guy.

I tried to rationalize. Class lists? What harm could there be in that? For one, the information is confidential. For identification purposes, each name has a student ID number. In the case of the American students it's the Social Security number. When we posted exam grades we used to use those numbers instead of names. Now because of confidentiality, we can't even do that. "It's confidential stuff," I protested.

"This is FBI business," Wilkins said.

What was he going to do if I refused? Get a subpoena for a class list? Cause me trouble with the department head and the dean of students? "I guess I can make you a copy," I said. "Just don't say you're paying me and depositing the money in a Bahamian bank."

It was an allusion to a KGB trick that got me pegged as a paid Soviet agent.

Wilkins may be a Yooper with a disarming laid back nature, but he's also a government employee. "No budget for that."

I took the class lists to the office copy machine and handed him a set. "That all?" I asked, expecting more and afraid of what he might say.

Wilkins studied the sheets before he folded them and put them in his pocket. "For now. Thanks Irvin." That rascal pronounced the W like a V, his subtle reminder of my Russian connection.

He was playing with me. That kind of teasing can be amusing as long as it's not sinister.

I couldn't avoid explaining something about my class lists. "You'll see that one of the three sections is all Chinese students. They have specific problems with pronunciation. They're eager, but don't know our idioms."

"And the other two sections?"

I hadn't met the classes yet. "Looks like a mixture. Couple of German names, some Scandinavians who probably know English better than I do, and a bunch of Mohammeds. You know, most Moslems are named Mohammed."

"Any Pakistanis?"

I didn't know.

"No Afghans?"

"I can't imagine any Afghan has the money to send his son to study in Michigan."

"How do you pronounce the Chinese names?" Wilkins asked.

"I don't. They usually assume American sounding names like Mike or John. You've probably heard some of those. You call for technical assistance for your computer, get connected to Bangalore and talk to someone whose working name is Larry but whose real name is mumbledypeg." I imitated the Indian accent. "Just what is your problem, Mr. Wilkins?"

Wilkins laughed. It made his handlebar mustache jiggle. "You should be a comedian, Irvin."

"So what are you going to do with the class lists?"

He didn't answer directly. "We'll be in touch. Or I'll send someone."

"Oh? Someone carrying a folded copy of the New York Times and speaking in pass words?"

"You've been reading spy novels again." Wilkins left.

Hell, my life is a spy novel except I'm no James Bond or Jason Bourne. I had the feeling that this was going to lead to trouble.

For more of books by Harley L. Sachs, here's the list of those currently available:

MYSTERY NOVELS

The Mystery Club Series

THE MYSTERY CLUB SOLVES A MURDER
First and most popular of the Mystery Club series. Mary Higgins finds the body of Dora Reed on the roof of the Plaza retirement building, notifies the police, then tells the Mystery Club. They assume several suspects: the manager of the Plaza, Dora's son Donald, or a Plaza employee. Dora's husband, Ed Sutherland, is in Hawaii on board the yacht Miss Chief with an all girl crew. Carrying on their own investigation, the Mystery Club finally suspects Sutherland, though he seems to have a perfect alibi. If they can prove it to their satisfaction, will a court ever convict him-- if he can be found somewhere in the Pacific?

THE MYSTERY CLUB AND THE DEAD DOCTOR
Second in the Mystery Club series. The Mystery Club consists of five elderly women who live at the Rose Plaza and discuss mysteries written by women. The Mystery Club ladies have no idea of the consequences when Viola Cartwright, their blind member, asks them to go over her Medicare bills. That leads to suspicion about the identity of her personal assistant, Dorothy Anderson, who turns out to be using a stolen identity. Viola's doctor runs a phony clinic owned by a member of the Russian Mafia. Soon the investigation of Medicare bills leads to murder and tragedy, stopped only by the courage of Mary Higgins.

THE MYSTERY CLUB AND THE HIDDEN WITNESS
Third in the Mystery Club series. The ladies of the Mystery Club discover one of the residents is a crook under WITSEC, the witness protection program. He apparently keeps dipping into the employee gift fund. The Mystery Club bands together to track down the missing money, but what they discover is danger.

THE MYSTERY CLUB AND THE SERIAL WIDOW

Fourth in the Mystery Club series. Caroline Kostinsky, new resident at the Rose Plaza, is a widow four times over and she's looking for a fifth husband in retired General Hardcastle, but when drunk she says she killed all of her husbands. Except for her confession, there's no evidence. Now what?

DELIVER ME FROM EVIL
Responding to a posted invitation for new members for the Mystery Club, Judge Ira Kahane and Ursula Besette show up. Ursula, at a turning point in her life as a new Rose Plaza resident, is interested in Wicca and Kabala. Roberta Nelson believes one should not suffer a witch to live. Judge Kahane tries to lead Ursula on the right path, but there is conflict and tragedy coming.

WHITE SLAVE
Sequel to *The Mystery Club Solves a Murder*. The appearance of Ed Sutherland's gold bracelet in a Portland pawn shop revives retired detective Casey's interest in the cold case. He doesn't know that Sutherland has been picked up and is a slave on a Korean fishing boat. Sutherland, penniless, without clothes or identification, is stranded in New Zealand. Can he find his way back to Portland and be somehow redeemed or face a death sentence for first degree murder?

The Irwin Glass Series

BETRAYAL
Prequel to *Retribution*. Irwin Glass, BA in Russian, MA in International Relations, has a promising career in the Foreign Service in Moscow until he is snared in a classic "honey pot" seduction. He's young and naïve, honest, always wants to do the right thing, but at every turn he is betrayed. The incident in Moscow destroys his career. He is accused of being a paid Soviet agent and is pursued by the consequences of his encounter with the KGB twenty years later. Some enemies never let go

RETRIBUTION
Sequel to *Betrayal*. Newly married to Ivy Hartshorn, Irwin Glass gets a dunning letter from the IRS for taxes on interest at the Washington, DC account he didn't think he had. It's a joint account with his missing birth daughter and the balance is huge. Assuming it's money Katya's KGB father of record, Vladimir Putinsky (now Putin) deposited for her living expenses, Irwin moves it to force her to contact him. But Ivy warns him that he is laundering money and the people it belongs to will come after him. Irwin's complicated life is catching up with him, but this time he will find retribution.

BURNT OUT

Irwin Glass is approached by FBI Agent Wilkins who asks for Irwin's lists of foreign students. Not satisfied he wants more and is looking for potential terrorists among the Moslem students. Gradually Irwin is sucked into the role of FBI informant on the Michigan Institute of Technology's Muslim Students' Association and the results are tragic.

THE IRWIN GLASS TRILOGY

All three Irwin Glass books in one package deal. The Irwin Glass Trilogy combines all three of the Irwin Glass Mysteries: "Betrayal," "Retribution," and "Burnt Out," following the chaotic career of Irwin Glass who began, in "Betrayal," as a state department clerk in Moscow only to be caught in a classic honey pot seduction. Betrayed at every turn, he was sent back to the United States in disgrace to try to start a new life. No such luck. His teaching career is upturned by the revelation that the Moscow seduction had a consequence in the form of a beautiful student Katya who claims to be his daughter. In "Retribution," Irwin's KGB nemesis is in the United States seeking political asylum, but in fact is fleeing the Russian Mafia with Irwin as quarry. After "Retribution," Irwin thinks he is home free of all that intrigue, but the local FBI agent has a hold on him and wants information about potential terrorists among Irwin's students at Michigan Institute of Technology. There are risks to being a reluctant FBI informant, and Irwin's reports may be misconstrued with tragic results. What Irwin and his wife really want is a normal life, but his mysterious Russian birth daughter Katya remains an enigma. Is she or isn't she?

Other Mysteries

MURDER BY MAIL

German exchange student Klaus Hitz is more interested in making money than in asking questions about his work assignment. He doesn't know that the industrialist father of his punk girl friend is using him in a terrorist conspiracy to kill everyone in the United States with a mass mailing of a scratch and sniff virus. The plot begins to unravel when a Polish nurse brings blood samples from Libya and alerts a CIA agent. While the CIA and FBI track down the terrorists, Klaus Hitz gradually figures it out. How can he avoid being murdered or imprisoned for being naive?

MURDER IN THE KEWEENAW

CIA agent recovering from Post traumatic Stress after failed missions in Finland and a divorce is fishing in Lake Superior when he snags a corpse. He thinks he has seen the girl before and his attempt to identify her leads him to a ring of deadly pornographers. It almost costs him his own life.

CONSPIRACY!
Technical writer Tom Godot can't believe his luck when CONSPIRACY!, the book he has co-written with the elusive Harold Stevenson, is a hit. The book details a plot to hijack communication satellites. As Tom crosses the country on his book tour, he is disturbed by people interested in early drafts and dogged by an NSA agent. Communicating by fax with his editor and by encrypted e-mail with the mysterious Stevenson, Tom reaches out in his loneliness to his California girl friend Sylvia Hanson who turns out to be a pivotal figure. There is another conspiracy, and Tom is part of it

THE GOLD CHROMOSOME
When Adam Rottman's childless Aunt Sadie Gold died, the eight cousins learned her estate was in an irrevocable trust, the proceeds going to Adam's sister Sarah while she lives. After Sarah's death, the money would go to the last surviving cousin. It's a fatal tontine Adam's lawyer brother Harold set up. Would the cousins kill each other for one million dollars? Sarah's car is found in the river, but not Sarah. That begins a series of mysterious deaths. Coincidence? Or Murder? Who will be next? Adam and his psychologist wife Deborah must stop the chain before he, too, is eliminated.

BEN ZAKKAI'S COFFIN
Born of a Jewish father and a Catholic mother, Herman Bachrach insists he has no religion, but he is drawn by circumstance into a holocaust vendetta over gold stolen by a Swiss bank from Jewish depositors. Seduced by a woman who calls herself Diana, no last name, Herman is suspected by detective Sheehan to be her murderer. Someone else wants him dead. His Jewish boss provides him with a lawyer, but sends him to Switzerland to finish the job "Diana" started. It's an assignment he can't refuse. The result is an epiphany of identity that changes Herman's life forever.

THE LOLLIPOP MURDER
A warning for wannabe novelists! What happens when a stable of neurotic novelists who live in their pseudonyms and are bound by iron clad contracts are invited aboard their miserly Florida publisher's yacht for the Miami Book Fair only to find that they have no hope of ever earning a dime of royalties for their books? All this as Hurricane Gerta threatens to sink the yacht at the dock. It's grounds for murder

NOVELS

SAM IN LOVE
A coming of age romance for mature young adults. U.S. Army life in
Europe in the 1950's was an equivalent of the Grand Tour of the
eighteenth century when young men traveled and sowed wild oats.
Marty, roommate of Sam Logan, a PFC draftee serving in the US Army
in Munich, Germany, says all Sam needs is to get laid. Sam is not a
virgin, but has a Midwestern ethic and believes in love. He doesn't
know quite what that is. No Casanova, Sam, through a series of
tentative encounters, thinks he's found the love of his life.

STOPRAPE.COM
        Native Yooper Kerstin Mikkola, is a TV broadcaster at WMUP
with offices at an old airport terminal. She works for Queen Annie, her
mentor and widow of the original station owner. What Kerstin would
like is to move up to a network job but she is unknown.
        A surprise arrival at the station is Imogene Michener who, as a
marine recruit, was raped by her training sergeant Carlos Wayne
Sauvenier. Imogene's traumatic case was blown off by her commander.
Suffering from extreme PTSD and discharged, Imogene set up the
StopRape.com web site, inviting other victims to post their stories for
the world to read. As a result of the web posting, Sauvenier has been
castrated by a gang of violent California Women Warrior bikers.
Interviewed on WMUP television without showing her own face,
Imogene persuades Kerstin to give her a copy of the recorded but
unedited interview, and places the revised pitch for her web site on
You-Tube. Now Kerstin is identified, and hate mail follows. Kerstin
wanted to be noticed, but not to be vilified by alleged rapists.

SCI-FI AND FANTASY

NEVER TRUST A TALKING HORSE
The narrator of this dystopian novel escapes preventive detention into a
world he discovers has gone mad. Hungry, he is told he can eat for
free at Lachumba's supper club, only to discover that he might be the
main dish. He rescues Iris I. Iris from the ovens and in a series of
episodes explores the insane world in search of a livelihood. He
gradually realizes why he was incarcerated in the first place, but by
then it is too late. His and Iris's roles have been reversed. Arrested,
they are given a sadistic sentence which is their final challenge.

THE SEARCH FOR JESSE BRAM

Jesse Bram, the young hero of this metaphysical science fiction adventure, is unaware of his Jewish roots. An Eldre of mixed breed, he is marooned on the post apocalyptic shunned planet URth where technology and books have been destroyed. The URthlings variously view Jesse as a bringer of cargo for the half-breed prefect Hrod, as the reborn Savior by crypto-Christians, and as a link to the past by a remnant of Jews. The Galactic Federation suspects him of treason and he is pursued by an enigmatic Trinian policeman. If Jesse survives, will he be convicted? If acquitted, what next?

SHORT STORIES

THREADS OF THE COVENANT: THE JEWS OF RED JACKET
A collection of twenty-one short stories about Jewish life in small town America centering about two main characters, David Katz, the only Jewish boy in Red Jacket, and Richard Goldman, the only Jewish professor at Copper country Community College. Each story depicts another aspect of what it means to be a Jew in a small town as each character comes to realize his own identity.

MISPLACED PERSONS
Though set in different locales what these stories have in common is a central character who is out of his element, in the wrong place, coming to grips with cultural, generational, or physical displacement. In PROBLEM FOR THE TEACHER an expatriate fumbles for a living; in LIMBO an ex-G.I. is adrift in Copenhagen; in TRIUMPH OF THE WILL a nervous wreck seeks recuperation; in MISCALCULATION a would be tax evader succumbs to his own fears; in THE LIE a drunk gets himself into difficulties, and in THE GIRLS OF FREDERIKSHAVN an old man is trapped by girls looking for action.

YOOPER TALES AND OTHER FUNNY STUFF
Extracted from the massive volume of Sachs's published Essays and Columns: 1992-2011, this collection of stories related to Michigan's Upper Peninsula, known as the UP, home of Yoopers, reveals the truth about snow fleas, ice worms, the humungous fungus (world's largest living thing) and the rigors of winters in the remote north woods. You can also learn how to catch and cook the Mosquito Giganticus and why visitors won't come. Sachs has several awards for his humor.

AHOY! QUARTERDECK!
Originally published as IRMA QUARTERDECK REPORTS but re-released with new illustrations and, in the paperback edition, with sea shanties, this funny book is a series of boating anecdotes about Irma

and her bumbling husband Ralph ("I can't believe I lost the anchor") Quarterdeck in their many boating adventures and mishaps. One reviewer says the book is as informative as Chapman's famous manual, but more fun. Readers will find plenty of laughs in this book and at the same time learn a great deal of boating fundamentals.

ANNA-LENA'S TROLL AND OHER STORIES
Each of the three Sachs daughters has a story in this children's book. "Anna-Lena's Troll" explores the nature of trolls, which represent the dark side of human behavior as Anna-Lena's nasty letter to Santa is rewarded by the gift of a nasty troll. "The Return of Baby Suzy" is the true story of Cynthia's worn out doll and its resurrection. "The Stars for Christmas" is the remarkable surprise Belinda got along with her new eye glasses. Other family stories are Christmas related.

NON-FICTION

THE MISADVENTURES OF CPL. SACHS
Adrift through college at Indiana University, author Sachs was drafted at the end of the Korean War. Physically unfit for combat, he was sent to Queer Company for basic training, then by a fluke was shipped out to Germany instead of Korea. Thus began his own version of the traditional Grand Tour.

FREELANCE NONFICTION ARTICLES
This third edition of a monograph on freelance writing first published by the Society for Technical Communication is newly updated. This little manual provides tips for interviewing, article structure, article preparation and submission, photography, and business practice.

CHILLY-CHILLY-BANG—HOW WE FREELANCED THROUGH EUROPE'S COLDEST WINTER IN A VW WITH A KID
Companion piece to *Freelance Nonfiction Articles*. The former is a how to book. This is a "how we did it" memoir. The author knew nothing about Volkswagens when they set off, but as they worked from VW dealer to dealer getting the old Combi fixed, he learned! It's as much a book for VW enthusiasts as it is for writers.

Both FREELANCE NONFICTION ARTICLES and *Chilly-Chilly-BANG! How we Freelanced Through Europe's Coldest Winter in a VW with a Kid* are combined in a double volume, *The Writing Life*.

THE 1957 SACHS ARCTIC EXPEDITION
After military service in Germany the author took the GI Bill to Sweden. With no income in the summer, and not even sure there was a

road to the far north, he set off hitchhiking to North Cape, the northernmost point in Europe in search of the midnight sun. Illustrated.

FROM TENT TO CASTLE: MEMOIR OF A YEAR LONG HONEYMOON

Setting off from Stockholm, Sweden on rebuilt one speed bicycles, Harley and Ulla embarked on an open-ended honeymoon with no fixed destination and equipped with a tent, a thin double sleeping bag, a tiny gasoline stove, and $3000. After arriving in Britain, Ulla discovered she was pregnant. Tired of unrelenting rain, they advertised for a cheap place to spend the winter. They were offered the gatehouse to Borthwick Castle outside Edinburgh, Scotland for $25 a month by British author Theo Lang.

"IS"

As Bill Clinton said, "It all depends on what the meaning of "is" is." A problem we all have is distinguishing between what is real and what is not. This is in fact an age-old question. This volume switches between classical instances of the problem to the author and his psychiatrist and his wife. What is real? That all depends on the meaning of "real."

QUEER COMPANY

Not a gay novel, this is a fictionalized memoir of an experimental basic training unit at the end of the Korean War. All the draftees were physically unfit for combat but the army didn't want to discharge them. Instead they got modified training in a company unfortunately designated Q. In the Army phonetic alphabet Q is Queen, but Q company was called queer. A copy is in the US Army historical archives.

www.ingramcontent.com/pod-product-compliance
Lightning Source LLC
Chambersburg PA
CBHW050840180626
46814CB00007B/2557